"You swear to me your friend is innocent?"

He looked her in the eye. "I swear it! I would trust him with my life, as I would any of our company."

"Very well." Lady Sarah nodded. "If anyone asks, I've ordered you to help me. Then when we're away from the house we can form a plan."

"A plan?" Ben echoed.

"Of course!" Lady Sarah's green eyes gleamed with excitement. "To get Solomon released. Which means that first we have to find out who really stole the Lodovico plate."

To Lisa, once again

First published in the UK in 2007 by Usborne Publishing Ltd., Usborne House, 83-85 Saffron Hill, London EC1N 8RT, England. www.usborne.com

Copyright © John Pilkington, 2007

The right of John Pilkington to be identified as the author of this work has been asserted by him in accordance with the Copyright, Designs and Patents Act, 1988.

Cover artwork by Ian Jackson. Map by Ian McNee.

The name Usborne and the devices ♀ ⊕ are Trade Marks of Usborne Publishing Ltd.

This is a work of fiction. The characters, incidents, and dialogues are products of the author's imagination and are not to be construed as real. Any resemblance to actual events or persons, living or dead, is entirely coincidental.

A CIP catalogue record for this book is available from the British Library.

J MAMJJASOND/07   ISBN 9780746078792   Printed in Great Britain.

ELIZABETHAN MYSTERIES

Rogues' Gold

John Pilkington

USBORNE

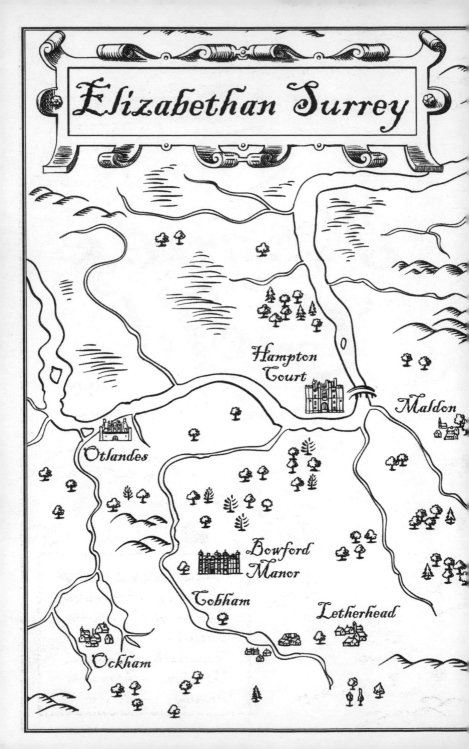

London

River Thames

Southwarke

Grenewich

Stretham

Towting

Croydon

Morden

Tadworth

Elizabethan place names

Grenewich – Greenwich
Letherhead – Leatherhead
Otlandes   – Oatlands
Southwarke – Southwark
Stretham   – Streatham
Towting   – Tooting

Chapter One

The hardest thing Ben Button had to do that morning, was say goodbye to Brutus.

Ben climbed up onto the cart, and sat beside his master, John Symes, on the driver's bench. He had already said goodbye to John's wife and daughters. They understood that John, Ben and the rest of the company would only be away for the summer. But Brutus was a dog, who didn't understand it at all.

Brutus stood outside the Symes's house, on the corner of Hog Lane, his tail and ears drooping sadly. John shook the reins, and the cart began to move off.

Brutus watched it roll away down Bishopsgate Street towards the city.

Ben was excited about going on tour for the first time, but the thought of leaving Brutus brought a huge lump to his throat. The old hound had been his friend since he'd first come to live at the Symes's house last winter. To leave him behind was almost more than Ben could bear. He bit his lip.

Soon they would pass under the stone arch of Bishopsgate and enter the city, and the house would be lost to sight... Ben looked back, and his heart thumped. Brutus was still there in the distance, watching the cart disappear. Before he knew what he was doing, Ben raised his hand and waved. And it seemed to him that the dog lifted his head, as if to show that he understood and didn't blame Ben too much after all. Feeling a little better, Ben turned and stared ahead at the horse's back.

Ben Button was a boy actor. He had been apprenticed to his master John Symes six months ago soon after his twelfth birthday. John was a fine character actor, and the chief musician of Lord Bonner's Men, who considered themselves the best acting company in London. To Ben, John was like a father: the father he no longer had, since Peter Button had died three summers ago, leaving Ben's mother struggling to bring up her three young children alone. Then, one day, John spotted Ben singing and dancing at a village summer fair. He knew at once that Ben's future lay with the stage, and Ben's mother agreed to an apprenticeship. Since then Ben had become close to John, as he had to all the actors of Lord Bonner's Men. They were like family now, and he wondered for a moment when he would see his real family – his mother, brother and sister – again.

Lord Bonner's troupe usually performed in any one of the open-air theatres that stood outside the city walls, north and south of the River Thames. But now with the summer coming on, everything had changed: the theatres were closed, and the acting companies had to look elsewhere for work, so Lord Bonner's Men were leaving London and going on tour. They were heading south, into Surrey. Ben had never been so far away in his life. It scared him a little – but it excited him, too.

The cart rattled on the cobbles as they rolled under Bishopsgate. Although it was still early morning, with the sun just beginning to climb above the rooftops, there were a lot of people about: carters and peddlers coming in to sell their wares, servants and housewives with covered baskets hurrying to the markets to buy. Ben, who came from the sleepy village of Hornsey a few miles north of London, where his father had been the blacksmith, always found the city a noisy, crowded place. And in the theatres, the crowds were at their noisiest and rowdiest: a mass of laughing, shouting, disorderly people. The first time he had stepped onto a stage, Ben had been terrified. He thought of it as they passed by the Cross Keys Inn in Gracious Street, which had a stage in the yard where the company sometimes performed. But now that he was a seasoned performer, Ben could smile about it. The theatre was his life, and he wanted no other.

To his left he could see the Tower of London, looming above the houses. He glanced at John, who was holding the reins and had said nothing since they left the house. John turned to him with a kindly look.

"He'll still be there when we get back," he smiled. "Brutus, I mean."

Ben nodded. The noise of the city filled his ears, as they rattled down Fish Street Hill. He saw the huge bulk of London Bridge ahead.

Emerging from the southern end of the great stone bridge, John drove the cart past the church of St. Mary Overies and halted. Here on Southwark shore the houses soon gave way to fields. The countryside of Surrey stretched away southwards.

There was a shout. A group of garishly dressed men stood some yards away, surrounded by a heap of baggage: chests of costumes and props, bundles of curtains and bits of scenery. A smile spread across Ben's face. The four actors waiting by the roadside made up the remainder of Lord Bonner's touring company. Excited, he clambered down from the cart to greet the first of them, a grinning, handsome man with long auburn hair, who stepped forward, picked Ben up and lifted him into the air.

"Hey, put me down!" Ben shouted, though he was laughing.

Hugh Cotton, the company's leading player and sword-fighting expert, set him down and pointed to the baggage. "Very well, Master Ben – but you'd best get to work!"

Ben helped with the loading as the company gathered about the cart. He struggled to lift a chest, and was frowned at by the oldest of the men, grumpy Will Sanders. Will was their jack of all trades: cook, prompter and supporting player, who took any parts that needed filling, from servants and soldiers to old men. Some said he looked better in a gown and a long grey wig than he did in his normal clothes.

"This trip's doomed – I hope you know that."

Ben turned to find himself looking into the gloomy

face of Solomon Tree, the tall, spindle-thin actor who specialized in comic roles. The first time he heard that, Ben thought the company were having a joke with him. Later on, he came to know better. Onstage, Solomon was a hoot; off it, however, he was hard work – that is, until Ben found a way to deal with him.

"Why is it doomed, Sol?" he asked in an innocent tone.

"A feeling in my bones..." Solomon shook his head slowly. "Heard a barn owl last night, behind my lodgings – no good can come of that."

Ben caught the twinkle in John Symes's eye as he passed by carrying boxes, but kept his face very straight. He let out a gasp. "A barn owl's bad enough – but are you sure it wasn't a loger owl?"

Solomon frowned at him. "Loger owl? Never heard of it."

Ben put a hand to his mouth. "We have them in the country, where I come from," he said in a voice of awe. "The old folk are terrified of them... They say they bring doom on anyone who hears them."

"No..." Solomon rubbed his stubbly chin. "It was a barn owl, I swear – couldn't be a loger." He gulped. "Could it?"

"I hope not," Ben answered gravely. "Otherwise I don't know what might happen." Over Solomon's shoulder he saw the others watching, trying not to laugh.

Solomon was looking quite worried now. "What sort of doom do they bring?" he asked.

Ben sighed and shook his head. "It could mean a dog's about to bite you," he said. When Solomon looked blank-faced, he added: "If you hear a low growl... Loger-owl, low growl. See?"

There was a snort of laughter. Solomon looked round to see the others grinning, and understood.

"That was cruel, young Ben," he said, shaking his head. "You had me worried."

Ben smiled, then looked apologetic. "Sorry, Sol. It was—"

"It was too easy." The last member of the company interrupted, putting a hand on Solomon's shoulder. He was a little, nervous man called Gabriel Tucker, who specialized in villain's roles. Ben had found it harder to get used to Gabriel than any of the others – especially the way his nervousness suddenly disappeared the moment he buckled on a sword or dagger.

"You never learn, do you?" Gabriel said. "You fall for Ben's puns every time."

The comic nodded. "Every time," he agreed gloomily. "Perhaps he should try my job, and match wits with the audience."

Ben shook his head. "I couldn't do what you do," he began, then yelped. Solomon had yanked him off his feet and was holding him upside down.

"There's a horse trough across the road," the comic said. "Seems to me you could do with cooling off..."

"No!" Ben kicked and squirmed like a rabbit. "Don't..."

There was laughter from the others, until John called a halt to the horseplay. "The sun's climbing," he said. "And we've a long walk ahead. Shall we make a start?"

Solomon lowered Ben onto the grass. "That's paid you," he said, his gloomy expression back in place. "Next time it's the trough."

"I'll remember," Ben said as he scrambled nimbly to his feet. But he was already grinning to himself. It wouldn't be long before he thought up another trick to play on Solomon.

The loading completed, they stepped into the roadway, while Will Sanders climbed onto the cart to take his turn at driving. He shook the reins and began to ease the carthorse forward. The old, chestnut-coloured horse was named Tarlton after a famous comedian who had died a few years before. It was another of the players' little jokes.

But as the company started on their way, there came a last word from Solomon Tree. "I still say the trip's doomed," he muttered. "Owl or no..."

The Surrey countryside rolled by all day, in the warm haze of early summer. Through woods, fields and small villages – Streatham, Tooting, Malden – Lord Bonner's Men tramped the dusty road, heading south-west towards the Downlands. The actors walked in front, while the cart brought up the rear. With only brief rest stops to take some bread and ale, and to feed and water Tarlton, they covered twenty miles, which seemed to Ben a huge distance. By evening London was far behind. As the shadows lengthened the players splashed through a small stream, climbed a hill and halted, all of them footsore and weary. Ben was sitting on the cart beside Will, falling asleep, when John's voice from ahead made him open his eyes.

"This brook flows into the River Mole," he called out. "That's Bowford Manor ahead. The town of Cobham's only a mile or two beyond."

Ben sat up and peered forward. In the distance he could make out a large stone house surrounded by outbuildings. Closer to, he could see horses in a fenced paddock. He knew Bowford Manor was the first stop on their tour – their patron Lord Bonner had arranged it. Though after that, the company would have to take their chances at the towns and villages along the way. Some would make them welcome, while others might not. It was a precarious sort of life, being a player.

Hugh looked back towards the cart with a grin. "How does supper and a soft bed sound?" he asked cheerfully.

The others brightened, and set off down the slope towards the welcoming sight. Wide awake now, Ben turned to Will, who sat hunched over the reins.

"Who's the master of Bowford Manor?" he asked.

Will grunted. "Sir James Howard," he answered. "One of the richest men in the county. They say he's quite a favourite at court."

Ben was quiet. Talk of Queen Elizabeth's court always bored him. Though he had caught glimpses of the Queen several times in her royal barge on the River Thames, he had never seen her close up. He knew, as most people did, that she was a gifted and clever woman, who had many suitors but had never married. Like her father, King Henry VIII, she loved music, sports and dancing, and she spoke several languages. She also loved the theatre, and Lord

Bonner's men had hopes that soon they would be called to entertain at one of her palaces. But apart from talk of the Queen herself, Ben seldom understood the gossip he overheard in theatres. It was usually about politics: who was in favour at court and who was not. He heard it mainly from the richly dressed gentlemen who sometimes sat on the stage, scoffing at the actors. Fetching stools for such people was the only part of his work Ben truly disliked. He hoped Sir James Howard's houschold was not like that.

Ben was about to ask Will another question, when from somewhere to the right came the blast of a hunting horn. The players stopped in surprise as a large deer crashed through the bushes, skidded into the road and veered away up the slope from where they had come. As it disappeared over the ridge, two riders appeared on sweating horses, in hot pursuit. But seeing the startled troupe of travellers and their cart in the way, the pair drew rein and halted.

The first was a bulky man with a black beard, wearing fine hunting clothes of dark brown and a feathered hat. Ben's eyes widened: surely this was a knight or earl – perhaps Sir James Howard himself? The big roan horse with its tooled harness suggested a man of wealth and status. As if to confirm this, the rider spoke up in a loud voice – which was far from friendly.

"What rabble is this?"

He sat his horse and stared at the players in their bright clothes. Hugh Cotton wore a duck-green doublet with the sleeves slashed to show the yellow silk lining, whereas John Symes favoured sky blue and a cocked hat to match. Gabriel's bright red cloak was slung over his shoulder and Solomon wore his customary red and yellow comedian's suit, next to which Ben's maroon doublet and baggy breeches appeared quite plain. Only Will, in his shirtsleeves, looked ordinary.

"I asked who you are!" the rider barked. "I'm not accustomed to having to repeat myself."

John stepped forward and removed his hat. "Lord Bonner's players, at your service, sir," he replied, and made his bow. "We are come to entertain Sir James Howard, at Bowford."

The man frowned. "I'm a guest at Bowford," he said. "And I know nothing of any players…"

At that, his companion eased his horse forward. He was an older man in plainer clothes, who took off his hunting cap to reveal a shining bald head. He looked down at John and the others and smiled. But to Ben it seemed an odd sort of smile; neither warm nor friendly.

"I'm Thomas Bullen, steward to Sir James," he said. "We did not expect you until tomorrow. You must have made good progress."

Lord Bonner's men began to relax. Players like them were always at risk on the road, which is why they had to have papers from a nobleman proving that they were authorized to travel and provide entertainment. Otherwise they could be arrested as rogues and vagabonds and thrown into jail, or even worse.

"We left London early, sir," John answered. "We have indeed had a hard day's march…"

"Then you'd better follow me down to the manor," Bullen replied. "A chamber is ready for you, I believe – and if you speak kindly to the cook, he will no doubt find you something to eat…"

He turned to his companion, who was growing impatient. "Sir Ralph," he began, but the haughty man tugged hard at the rein, making his horse jerk its head in alarm. Ben found himself disliking this noble personage more by the minute.

"I've a deer to hunt, Master Bullen," the man retorted. "And I have been delayed long enough!"

And with that he dug his heels into the horse's flanks and galloped away. In a moment he had ridden over the crest of the hill and out of sight.

Thomas Bullen turned to the players. "Sir Ralph has had a poor day's sport," he said smoothly. "He's a man who takes his pleasures seriously. Now…" He gestured towards the distant house. "Shall we proceed?"

The players nodded, and began the last part of their journey. But as Will started Tarlton forward, Ben found his eyes resting upon the bald-headed steward ahead of them. Ben wasn't quite sure why, but he disliked Master Bullen, even more than the angry-looking Sir Ralph. Then he decided it must be the man's smile: it reminded him of the grinning jaws of a hunting dog, before it stoops for the kill.

Chapter Two

Two hours later all thoughts of his journey had been driven from Ben's mind, as he and the rest of Lord Bonner's Men appeared from behind a curtain in the great hall of Bowford Manor.

It was the most splendid place Ben had ever seen. Light blazed from the many candles that hung overhead and reflected from the gold and silver goblets and plates on the tables. The audience, in rich silk clothes and wearing a lot of jewels, sat on three sides of the long room. As the players hurried out, they broke into loud applause. Forming a line, the company made their bows, then launched into their opening song, "Fine Knacks for Ladies".

John played the lute, which had taken him the past hour to tune. Gabriel and Hugh had recorders, while Solomon carried a drum around his neck. After playing a lively opening, they all sang while Ben and Will hurried to set the stage: a throne for the king at one side, a cleared space for sword fighting at the other. The song ended to cheers and more applause, but the company quickly put aside their instruments as John stepped forward. In ringing tones he announced that the play they would now perform was *The Massacre at Paris*, by the famous playwright Kit Marlowe.

The Massacre was an exciting play, with fights and murders but also with fine speeches. Only an experienced company like Lord Bonner's would attempt it, for they must take over thirty parts between them, disappearing behind the curtain to change a hat or wig, to grab a cloak or sword and hurry out again.

Behind the curtain was the tiring room – the actors' changing area. While he changed, Ben peered through the curtain, watching Hugh's sword-fight with Gabriel, which always looked more dangerous than it actually was. As the only boy actor, he had to take all the women's parts: that was his job. One moment he was the Queen of Navarre in fine robes and a crown; the next he was Catherine the old Queen Mother in a white wig, leaning on a stick. The play moved so fast, he barely had time to change or remember his lines – but that also meant there was no time to feel nervous. In fact he was concentrating so hard he forgot all about the audience until the very end of the performance. Then, tired but happy, he joined the others in taking his bow, to deafening applause.

Now, at last, he dared to look out at the forty or fifty gentlemen, ladies and attendants who were all on their feet, shouting for more. To his left he saw Hugh in his duke's costume, bowing and smiling. Even Will and Solomon were grinning... He felt John's hand squeeze his shoulder, and knew that he was pleased with Ben's performance.

Ben smiled and bowed again. The weariness in his limbs after the long day's journey slowly returned, but in his exhilaration Ben barely noticed. He was Ben Button, boy actor: a success. He would sleep deeply that night, in the soft bed he had been promised...and in the morning...

Let the morning take care of itself, he thought. After following the others back to the tiring room, he

sat down on a hamper of costumes, yawned once –
and fell fast asleep.

But much later, as dawn was breaking, Ben woke
with a start, breaking a dream about owls. He had a
vague memory of being carried upstairs to a sleeping
chamber. Now, he saw the door open, and heard
voices. For a moment he had forgotten where he was
– then he sat bolt upright, as someone appeared
holding a torch. The other men of Lord Bonner's
company, lying on straw pallets on the floor, were
also waking up. But before anyone could ask what
was going on, several heavy-looking figures came
stamping into the room – and now there was no
mistaking the clank of swords. Not knowing what to
do, Ben leaped to his feet, but at once a hard voice
called out, "Stay where you are!"

The torch was lifted high, showing men-at-arms in
Sir James Howard's scarlet livery, standing grim-
faced in a semicircle. Then a shorter figure with a
bald head that shone in the torchlight came forward;
and Ben's heart sank.

"Where is the comedian – the tall fellow?"

Thomas Bullen was wearing the same thin smile he
had worn the day before by the roadside. Ben looked
into his eyes, and saw nothing there but cruelty.
Bullen stared at each of the startled players in turn.

But as John began to rise, as if to make some protest, the steward held up a warning hand. At the same time Solomon, whose bed was against the opposite wall, got slowly to his feet.

"I suppose I'm the one you mean... My name's Tree."

Bullen gestured to the nearest man to move his torch, so it lit up poor Solomon in his nightshirt. He stood blinking in the light.

The steward's gaze swept the room, then settled once again upon Solomon. "You're under arrest," he snapped. "For theft!"

As the players gasped he raised his hand again, and he was no longer smiling. "If any of you try to hinder me, you too will be arrested," he said, and turned to the guards.

"Take him away!"

At once they stepped forward, took hold of a speechless Solomon, and bustled him roughly out of the door. In a moment they were gone, and the room fell into darkness.

For about a minute, nobody spoke. Then there was a spark of flame, as John struck a light from his tinderbox. He found a torch in a holder fixed to the wall, and lit it. Shocked, the rest of the company gathered about him. Ben found that his heart was thumping.

"Theft...?" Hugh said, shaking his head. "It's a mistake. It must be! Solomon never stole anything in his life."

Gabriel looked even more nervous than usual. "But if something has been stolen, the first people they'll blame are travelling players like us. We're always looked on as rogues!"

Will was frowning. "That steward – Bullen – he came straight in looking for Sol. Why would he do that?"

Nobody had an answer. It seemed too incredible for words. They sat on their beds, each one busy with his own thoughts. After a while the sun came up, its rays poking through the windows of the chamber. Slowly and solemnly the players rose and began to get dressed. Ben, the first to be ready, caught John's eye and saw how worried he looked.

"Does this mean we'll have to stay here, at Bowford Manor?" Ben asked. "We can't leave Solomon behind..."

"Of course we can't." John took a deep breath, and looked round at the others. "The first thing we're going to do is demand to see Sir James himself," he announced. "We'll ask him what's going on, instead of hearing it from that smirking steward of his."

Ben's heart lifted. John was a gentle man but a brave one, who would stand up to the entire Queen's Privy Council if he had to. He glanced round to see that the others seemed as cheered as he was. Only Will showed his usual grumpiness.

"D'you think they'll still give us breakfast?" he asked.

It was late in the morning before Lord Bonner's Men were at last allowed an audience with Sir James Howard. They were not shown into the great hall but into a smaller chamber at the front of the house. Sun streamed through the windows onto a long table scattered with papers. Stern-looking servants stood round the walls. Seated behind the table, like a row of judges, were Sir James and his wife Lady Anne, and Thomas Bullen the steward. There was also a boy, two or three years older than Ben, dressed in a fine doublet of purple silk. As Ben entered he felt the boy's eyes upon him, and saw the sneer of disdain. He met the other's gaze without flinching, and felt he had won a small victory when the boy at last looked away.

Sir James, whom Ben had barely glimpsed among

last night's audience, was something of a surprise. Instead of the imposing figure he expected, the master of Bowford was a small, pale man with sandy hair and a reddish beard. His wife Lady Anne was taller, a dark-haired woman with her face painted in the Queen's fashion: a foundation of white lead paste with bright red lips. Her blue gown was very fine and glittered with jewels. Her husband in his black doublet and breeches looked almost plain beside her, except that he wore a white starched ruff and a gold chain on his chest.

The actors lined up before the table. Gabriel coughed nervously, and Will was grunting into his beard, but John and Hugh acted like the noblemen they had played in *The Massacre at Paris*. After a moment, Sir James settled his gaze upon John.

"What is it you wish to say, Master Symes?"

John took a breath. "We are deeply shocked, sir, at the arrest of one of our company," he answered. "We know him well, and he's no thief – I swear it. We can only think there has been some mistake—"

"How dare you!" Bullen was glaring at them. "You're nothing but common players, little more than vagabonds...do you challenge Sir James's authority?"

"Of course not." John faced him calmly. "But if we

might know what's been stolen, and why Solomon has been accused, we might find some explanation..."

Bullen opened his mouth again, but Sir James lifted a hand. "The matter is very grave," he said. "A valuable piece of gold plate, that has been in my family for some years, is missing. It was on the high table last night in full view of everyone, including yourselves..." He looked at each of them in turn. "I need hardly remind you that theft of such an object is a serious felony, punishable by death."

There was a stunned silence. And before John could reply, Lady Anne Howard spoke.

"Your comedian gave a charming performance last night." Her voice was gentle, but somehow it made Ben feel uncomfortable. "Even here in the country we have heard of Master Tree," Lady Anne went on. "He is well known for his tricks, is he not – hiding things under his coat, for example? It saddens me to think him a thief. Yet he was seen to eye the plate when he took his bow...a greedy look, someone said. There would have been ample time, when our guests had gone to their beds and the servants were clearing the hall, for him – or indeed, any of you – to slip in and..." She shrugged. But the accusation was clear enough.

A sneering voice chimed in: that of the haughty-looking boy at the end of the table. "I thought the company's performance poor, Mother," he said to Lady Anne. "They're just a parcel of rogues – send them away, and let the law deal with the guilty one."

The players looked alarmed, but Sir James spoke up. "No one asked your opinion, Giles," he said in a tired voice. "What happens to these men is my decision."

"Indeed, sir…" Lady Anne turned to her husband with a faint smile. "But Giles, keen-eyed as always, is voicing the views of the household. All at Bowford – guests as well as servants – are trusted, down to the lowest scullery maid. The thief is caught, so why let these interlopers remain a moment longer?"

Ben, his heart sinking, glanced at John and saw him downcast. But Hugh fixed Lady Anne with one of his charming smiles, and spoke up.

"My Lady, you are distressed by this terrible theft, as anyone would be. But let me assure you of our goodwill, indeed of our desire to help. If a search is to be made—"

"Silence!"

Thomas Bullen was on his feet. "Your insolence will not be borne, fellow!" he snapped. "A thorough search has already been made of the house and grounds, and nothing was found. It remains for the thief to tell where he has hidden the plate. And he will confess it sooner or later, believe me!"

The actors froze, but Sir James was looking at Bullen, as if he disapproved of the outburst. After a moment the steward bowed to his master and sat down. Sir James addressed the actors again.

"You will all remain here for the present," he said, "since the constable from Cobham may wish to question you." He hesitated. "I know your patron, the noble Lord Bonner, whose seal is on your warrant. I'll send word to London, and advise him of what has happened. Meanwhile you may take your meals in the kitchens with the other servants, and not stray from the house until I order otherwise. Is that clear?"

The players glanced at each other, but there was nothing more to say. Hugh and John exchanged looks, then bowed to their host. The others did the same. Sir James, Lady Anne and Bullen sat in silence as they filed sadly out of the doorway.

The last to leave, Ben could not resist a quick glance behind – to see Giles staring coldly at him again. Uneasily, he followed the others out, thinking of Solomon. If Sol was not proved innocent of this theft, then what was going to happen to him?

Chapter Three

The players went back to their chamber, on the first floor of the great house. They sat upon their beds for much of that day like prisoners, except the door was not locked. It seemed there was nothing they could do. John had sent a request through Master Lamb the cook, a fat man who seemed to bear them no particular grudge, that they be allowed to visit Solomon. But the request was denied by Thomas Bullen, and worse, nobody would even tell them where Solomon was.

In the afternoon, feeling restless, Ben asked if he

might go outside. John hesitated, then gave him a kindly smile.

"They can hardly object to your taking a little exercise," he said. "What harm can you do? You go – and if anyone asks, say you're on an errand for us."

"Perhaps I could try and find out where they're holding Sol," Ben said.

The others nodded, though none of them seemed to hold out much hope.

It was mid-afternoon, and there was hardly anyone about. Nobody challenged Ben as he walked down the stone stairway, along a passageway and out through an open door. He stopped at the side of the house beside a path. There was a high stone wall on the other side. Not having any plan, he began to follow the path. Ahead he could see gardens, stretching away to a paddock where horses grazed.

Then came a voice, which stopped him in his tracks.

"Stay where you are, or I'll shoot!"

Ben froze. The voice had come from behind him, but it was not a grown-up's; in fact, it sounded like a girl's. Slowly he turned round.

At first he saw no one. Then a movement caught his eye, and he looked up to see a small head poking above the wall. Whoever it was must be standing on something, since the wall was at least six feet high.

"I said stay there!" the girl called. As Ben watched, a foot in a green leather shoe appeared. The next minute the girl had scrambled over the wall, jumped down and walked towards him, slightly out of breath.

They stared at each other. She was about Ben's age, though shorter than him. She wore a plain gown of bottle green over a white kirtle that was stained with dirt and torn at the edge. Her red hair, though styled after a fashion, had come loose from its pins in several places.

"What did you mean, you'll shoot?" Ben asked – then saw that the girl was holding a toy bow made from a willow sapling, with a small arrow in it. As he looked, she raised and pointed it. But to her dismay, Ben almost laughed.

"What do you think that would do?"

"It can stick in your chest," the girl answered stoutly. "The point's made from sharp bone."

Ben smiled, then reached out, grabbed the arrow and snapped it. The girl loosed the bowstring, but it twanged uselessly.

"Rogue!" She stepped back. "I should have known you for a villain – whatever Master Henry says!"

"Who's Master Henry?" Ben asked, and handed her the broken arrow.

"My tutor," the girl answered, then added: "I could report you, and have you locked up like that other fellow!"

"You pointed the bow," Ben said, frowning. "I haven't done anything wrong, and neither has Solomon – it's all a mistake!"

The girl looked at him closely. "I saw you perform last night," she said. "You look better in boy's clothes than you do in those silly dresses."

Ben blushed red in the face. "I play other parts than women," he began, then saw the look of amusement in her eyes.

"What are you doing here?" she asked.

"What business is it of yours?" he countered. He had decided that this scruffy-looking girl was probably one of the servants, though he'd never heard of a servant having a tutor.

"Such insolence!" The girl's eyes widened. "You're either a very brave boy, or a very stupid one."

"I'm not stupid," Ben retorted.

The girl hesitated. "Do you want to see Tamora?" she asked suddenly.

"Who's Tamora?"

"My pony, of course. She's named after the ancient Queen of the Goths."

35

Ben must have looked puzzled, because the girl laughed. "Follow me," she said, and turned on her heel. Not knowing what else to do, he followed.

The girl led him round the corner of the wall, along another path and through an archway, until at last Ben realized where he was. The arch gave on to a big cobbled yard which smelled of horse manure. He could hear the animals stamping and snorting in their stables.

They passed through a doorway into darkness. As Ben's eyes adjusted to the gloom he heard a whinnying, and looked round to see the girl standing beside a beautiful, dappled-grey pony.

"This is Tamora."

Ben walked forward, reached out and stroked the pony's nose gently. Tamora blinked at him, then snickered softly.

"She likes you," the girl said in a surprised voice. "She doesn't usually take to strangers."

Ben realized now that this girl was no ordinary servant. It had occurred to him that she might be pretending the horse was hers. But Tamora turned her head towards the girl, and allowed herself to be stroked. As Ben tried to think things out, the girl saw his discomfort and smiled. "You don't know who I am, do you?"

He shook his head.

There was a loud snort from some yards away. Ben turned and almost shouted. Tethered to a ring in the wall, was a big chestnut horse...

"Tarlton!" He ran forward and put his arm round the familiar neck, taking hold of Tarlton's thick mane. The old horse knew him at once, and grunted in reply.

"He's ours," Ben explained to the girl. "He draws the cart, when we go travelling."

"We can feed him, if you like," she said.

And as Ben watched, she went to a manger which stood against the far wall, plunged her hands in and drew out an armful of hay. Ben went over and did the same. As they brought the hay to Tarlton he jerked his head, stamped, then opened his huge jaws and took a mouthful. From the greedy way he ate, it was clear that he hadn't been fed all day.

"How could they neglect him like this?" Ben asked hotly. "He's just a horse – he hasn't done anything..."

"Oi! What do you think you're doing!"

Ben turned sharply, as heavy boots scraped on the cobbles. A man stood framed in the doorway, pointing a finger at him.

"You little runt – I'll leather you! You've no right..."

The groom took a step towards Ben. But the next

moment a voice cried out, echoing to the rafters.

"Are you responsible for the care of this horse?"

The man saw the girl, and stopped dead. "My Lady…" He faltered. Ben stiffened too, realizing his serious mistake. This girl was clearly not a servant at all.

"I asked you a question!" she demanded, and the man gulped.

"I'm responsible, yes…"

"Then why hasn't he been fed?"

The man wet his lips, as if his mouth had suddenly gone dry.

"Orders, from Master Bullen."

"Orders?" The girl stood quivering with anger. "Well I'm giving you a new order: from now on this horse will be fed and watered regularly. Or you will answer to my father!"

"As you say, My Lady…" The man nodded.

"Now you may go," the girl said. The fellow made a clumsy bow and turned away. But as he reached the doorway she called after him: "And this boy has my permission to come here – in fact, to go anywhere he pleases. Is that clear?"

The groom threw her a nod, and hurried outside.

Ben's heart was pounding like hoof-beats. But before he could open his mouth, the girl faced him.

"I'm Lady Sarah Howard, daughter of Sir James Howard."

Ben swallowed. "I'm sorry if I was rude, My Lady," he began, but Lady Sarah merely shook her head.

"I wouldn't really have reported you," she said.

Now that she had told him who she was, Ben saw a resemblance to Sir James Howard in her hair colour, and about the eyes, which were a deep shade of green like her gown. But in other ways, Lady Sarah was so unlike the rest of her family – especially her older brother – that he could think of nothing to say. He lowered his eyes and went on feeding hay to Tarlton.

"What did you say his name was?" Lady Sarah asked.

Ben told her, and at once she smiled. "After Dick Tarlton, the Queen's jester!"

"I think Dick Tarlton was her jester once," Ben agreed. "But my master knew him as one of the Queen's players..."

"Your master?"

"John Symes – he's the leader of our company. I'm his prentice..." He took a step back, and bowed. "Ben Button, player and servant to Lord Bonner, My Lady, at your service."

Lady Sarah smiled. "Ben Button...it's a nice

name." She thought for a moment. "Do you have duties today, Master Ben?"

"I've nothing to do but twiddle my thumbs all day – none of us has. We're stuck indoors like prisoners – though not like poor old Solomon…"

"Who?"

"Solomon Tree, our comedian – the one your father has had arrested," Ben told her. "Or rather, his steward has. Though Sol hasn't stolen anything – he wouldn't! He's as honest as any man!"

There was a silence, broken only by Tarlton munching hay.

"I'm sorry, My Lady," Ben went on, remembering his manners. "I mean no slight to your father. But there's been some terrible mistake, and Solomon is paying a cruel price for it."

Lady Sarah said nothing for such a long time that Ben began to feel uncomfortable. He wondered if he had offended her, but her next words startled him.

"You swear to me your friend is innocent?"

He looked her in the eye. "I swear it! I would trust him with my life, as I would any of our company."

"Very well." Lady Sarah nodded, as she walked over to her pony. "You can come with me while I exercise Tamora. If anyone asks, I've ordered you to help me. Then when we're away from the house we can form a plan."

"A plan?" Ben echoed.

"Of course!" Lady Sarah's green eyes gleamed with excitement as she untied Tamora's halter. "To get Solomon released. Which means that first we have to find out who really stole the Ludovico plate. And to do that we have to find the plate. It must be hidden somewhere."

A glimmer of hope began to form in Ben's mind, then it faded a little. "But Master Bullen said a search has already been made—"

Lady Sarah snorted. "Him? I wouldn't take his word that water's wet." She lowered her eyes, and a sad look came over her face. "This is not a happy household," she said quietly. "And if I can set you and your friends free, I will."

Her words took Ben by surprise. Unable to think what to say, he watched as Lady Sarah led Tamora out into the yard, the pony's hooves ringing on the cobbles. Ben followed her. The next moment she was running, leading Tamora by the long rein, through the gateway towards the paddock. And he had to hurry to catch up with her.

Things at Bowford Manor were more complicated than he had realized. If someone else had stolen the valuable plate, who could it be? And why was Solomon being blamed?

But most important of all was Lady Sarah's idea of a plan to save Sol... Surely it couldn't be as easy as that?

Chapter Four

They climbed a hill above the paddock, a long way from the house where nobody could overhear them. Then letting Tamora loose to graze the lush grass, Lady Sarah sat down and signalled Ben to sit beside her. She pointed towards the west.

"Our lands reach all the way down the valley, to the River Mole," she said. "That's Cobham in the distance."

"Your father said the constable from Cobham is coming to question us," Ben said. "About the theft – I mean, the loss of that plate."

Lady Sarah looked grave. "Then we must move fast. He's a friend of Master Bullen's, and I wouldn't trust him either. He's called William Piggott – I call him The Pig."

Ben's face clouded. "What do you think is going to happen?"

"One thing at a time," Lady Sarah answered. "First we have to form our plan."

He frowned. "Is it really valuable, the –"

"The Lodovico plate." Lady Sarah nodded. "Truly it is. It was a gift from the Scottish ambassador to my father when he was at court. It's not for eating off. It's gold, engraved and set with precious stones."

"Then why was it out in the hall last night, in full view? Why wasn't it locked safely away somewhere?"

"You don't know my stepmother, Lady Anne," replied Lady Sarah. "She likes to show everyone how rich we are, as if they didn't know already."

"Your stepmother?" Ben looked surprised.

"Sir James is my father," she explained. "My mother died when I was born. He was still a young man, and soon after he married Lady Anne. Her husband was dead, and she had a boy of her own."

"So Master Giles isn't your real brother?" Ben enquired, which prompted a snort.

"Of course he isn't! He's my stepbrother and he hates me!"

Ben fell silent. He had almost forgotten that she was Lady Sarah, and he a boy actor. Perhaps he ought to mind his manners, he thought; then he noticed how sad she looked.

"I hardly seem to see my father these days," she said, almost to herself. "Lady Anne always stops me, saying he's tired, or something." Lady Sarah sighed then. "If only father would see them for what they are," she went on. "He lets them do as they like!"

"You mean Lady Anne and Giles?" Ben asked.

She nodded. "Lady Anne wants my father to make Giles his heir, so he inherits everything." She looked up at Ben. "This has been our family home for centuries...to think of Giles being the master here, strutting about like a peacock, makes my blood boil!"

Ben didn't know what to say. But Lady Sarah took a deep breath, and smiled at him. "Let's forget my troubles. Yours are more urgent," she said, getting quickly to her feet. "There's someone who might help – someone we can trust: Master Henry."

"Your tutor?" Ben frowned. His own memories of school back home in Hornsey village were not very pleasant. "How could he help?"

"I'm not sure yet – but he's the cleverest man I

know," Lady Sarah told him. She walked over to where Tamora was cropping the grass, and caught up her halter. "Come on – we'd better get back before we're missed."

Together they walked downhill to the paddock. But as they opened the gate to lead Tamora through, there came a shout and the thunder of hooves. Both turned as a man on a big roan horse galloped up. At once Ben recognized him as the one who had chased the deer into the road, the day before.

"Uncle Ralph..." Lady Sarah stood beside Tamora, and made her curtsey.

The man looked down at them sternly. "Sarah, what on earth are you doing, alone with that boy?"

"He was helping me exercise my pony," Lady Sarah replied.

"But don't you know who he is?"

"Of course – he's one of the players. Please don't worry – after he's seen to my horse I'll send him back to the house. The grooms are nearby, so I'm not in any danger."

Sir Ralph hesitated. "Very well, but take no chances. They're all rogues – even the youngest of them!" And with a hard look at Ben, he spurred his horse forward and rode away.

Lady Sarah watched him go. "He isn't my real

uncle," she said. "He's Sir Ralph Gosson, Lady Anne's brother. He comes to stay with us sometimes." Suddenly she turned to Ben. "I know where they've put your friend, Master Tree."

"Where?" Ben asked sharply.

"In the brewhouse." Then she added: "We'll have to be careful, or someone will see us."

"Wait a minute!" Ben blurted out. "You mean to go there now, in broad daylight...?"

She stiffened. "Are you a coward, Ben Button?"

Ben felt the blood rise to his face. "No, I'm not."

"Then prove it." And without another word, she let go of Tamora's rein and walked quickly away across the paddock.

Ben closed the gate and followed her. Thoughts were buzzing about in his head like bees; but the main one was that he would never understand someone like Lady Sarah in a hundred years.

The brewhouse was a stone building that stood by itself at the corner of the kitchen garden. Gardeners were working some distance away between rows of peas and beans, but no one seemed to notice Ben and Lady Sarah as they walked up to the building. There was a stout door before them.

"It's locked," Lady Sarah whispered, and led the way round the corner. Here was a small window which was open but barred.

Ben glanced around. Luckily they were hidden from the house and gardens. Behind them were woods, from which birds chirped loudly. "How do you know he's in here?"

For answer, she rapped on the window frame. At once, there came a muffled sound from within. And to Ben's relief a familiar face loomed up, peering at them through the bars.

"Solomon!"

Solomon Tree stared, then his mouth dropped open. "Ben...?"

"Are you all right?" Ben asked anxiously. "They haven't hurt you or anything?"

Solomon shook his head, and his normal gloomy expression was back. "No, but I'm fettered – look!"

There came a clank of iron, as Solomon raised his arms. His wrists were chained together – and there was a longer chain leading away. Peering into the semi-darkness, Ben saw it led to a heavy ring set in the stone wall.

He swallowed. This was no time to show how upset he was: he must be as brave as he could, for Solomon's sake. He tried to smile. "Please don't worry, Sol. We'll get you out of there. It's all a misunderstanding, and it'll soon be put right. We're working on a plan, even now!"

Solomon got himself as close to the bars as he could, until the chain tethering him to the wall was drawn tight.

"I'm not a thief," he said hoarsely. "I don't even know what it is I'm supposed to have stolen. Tell John to speak with Sir James!"

"We're doing everything we can," Ben told him, feeling thoroughly useless. "And when Lord Bonner hears about it..."

But Solomon shook his head. "There isn't time. They're going to sweat me, and soon. I heard that steward fellow say it. And I know what that means: torture!"

Ben's heart missed a beat. Then he felt Lady Sarah tugging at his sleeve. "We must go, before somebody sees us," she said.

For the first time, Solomon noticed her. "Who's that?"

"A friend – she's helping me," Ben told him, making an effort to put on a brave face. "No one's going to sweat – I mean hurt you, Sol," he said, struggling to ignore the lump in his throat. "I said we'll get you out, and I mean it. In fact, it's a promise!"

Solomon sighed. "I told you this trip was doomed, didn't I?"

Unable to bear looking at poor Solomon any longer, Ben raised his hand in farewell and walked away. Tears blurred his eyes as he followed Lady Sarah through the garden and back to the stable yard. He went inside, to the welcome gloom of the stable, and found Tarlton. Lady Sarah left him alone, to tell his troubles to the old horse; and he hardly noticed that she was gone.

Soon afterwards Ben went back into the house through the same door he had used earlier. The other players quickly got to their feet as he entered their chamber. He told them all about his expedition, ending up with an account of Solomon's plight.

Hugh looked grave. "We don't know if Lord Bonner will come in time – or even if the message will reach him. How can we trust Sir James to send news, as he said he would?"

"I believe Sir James is a man of his word," John said, and turned his gaze upon Ben. "Meanwhile we owe our young prentice thanks, for the news that Solomon's unharmed – at least for the present."

Gabriel was looking anxious as usual. "Sir James's

daughter...do you think we can trust her?"

Ben thought for a moment. "Yes, I do." He sat down on a pallet, thinking of Lady Sarah. He believed that, like her father, she too was someone who would keep her word. After a while the others left him alone and began talking among themselves. They were still talking an hour later, when a servant came and told them to come down to the kitchens for supper.

And it was there in the huge, stone-flagged kitchen, which was unbearably hot from its roaring fire, that a surprising thing happened. A servant in Bowford livery approached the table where they ate. The man looked them over, then settled his gaze upon Ben.

"You're Master Button?"

Ben nodded.

"I have instruction for you. Sir James is displeased that someone so young should be spending his time in idleness. In his generosity, he will permit you to attend Lady Sarah tomorrow at her lessons, as a temporary pageboy. Be there at eight o'clock – and wash your face first!"

The man stalked off, leaving the players looking round in surprise. But Ben was silent, because he knew at once that Lady Sarah had spoken to Sir

James and persuaded him to let Ben go out tomorrow. Hope sprang in his heart, as he realized that she meant to keep her word, and help him form a plan.

Chapter Five

The next morning, having put on a clean shirt and his best doublet, Ben was taken to a high chamber at the rear of the house. There, sitting at a small desk by a window, was Lady Sarah. Today she wore a dark-blue gown, and her hair was dressed elaborately, with an embroidered caul on top. Ben bowed nervously, unsure who else might be in the room. And he had not long to wait to find out.

"Ah! Is this he?"

Ben looked round, but could see no one. The voice was high and reedy, like an old man's, but somehow he knew its owner wasn't old. It came from behind a huge pile of books on a table in the corner. Lady Sarah smiled at Ben.

There was a shuffling noise and a cough. "Has he a tongue in his head?"

Ben spoke up. "Yes, I have…" He trailed off, then added: "sir."

The pile of books lurched to one side and crashed to the floor, making a cloud of dust. A figure appeared at once, coughing and waving his hands about. On his nose were round spectacles, through which he squinted at Ben. "So, you're the boy player. You made a fine Queen of Navarre the other night."

"Thank you, sir," Ben said. The man was thin and bony with straggly blond hair and a pointed beard. He wore a dusty black doublet with holes at the elbows.

Lady Sarah stood up. "This is Henry Godfrey," she told Ben. "My tutor. He was Giles's tutor too, but we no longer have lessons together."

Henry Godfrey snorted. "That boy – I cannot teach him! He thinks he knows everything!" He eyed Ben suspiciously. "Are you one of that sort?"

Ben blinked. "I don't think so, Master Henry…"

"Good!" The tutor came closer, and looked round the room before lowering his voice. "I know of your plight," he said. "And I am troubled. For I think you are caught up in matters more dangerous than you imagine."

Lady Sarah spoke up. "My father's agreed that you wait upon me while you are here," she told Ben. "That way, we can come and go as we please. For it will be up to you and I to find the Lodovico plate."

Ben frowned. Things seemed to be getting more serious by the minute. But Master Henry seemed to understand, and gave him a kindly look. "I'll help if I can," he said. "But make no mistake: your friend Tree is in real danger!"

Ben was shaken. "I don't understand," he said. "Why do they keep Solomon locked up? How can he confess where he hid the plate, when he didn't steal it in the first place?"

The tutor looked Ben in the eye. "A man may confess to anything, under torture. He will say whatever they wish him to say." Ben's jaw dropped, but Henry went on: "It's my belief there's more to this than the mere theft of a valuable gold object. And if I'm correct, the last thing the real thief wants is for the plate to be found. Indeed, unless you can move swiftly, I think it will leave Bowford for good!"

Lady Sarah looked grave. "I think it's time you told us more, Master Henry," she urged.

Henry hesitated, peering at Ben. "I hope our trust in the boy is well-founded," he said.

"I trust him," Lady Sarah said, turning her gaze upon Ben, who blushed.

"I swear I'll do anything you and Lady Sarah ask," Ben told Henry. "I only want to see Solomon set free, so our company can leave here and be safely on our way."

"Very well." Henry Godfrey nodded. He gave a little sigh. "Before I came here as tutor," he began, "I was in the service of Lord Montagu, at his great country house of Cowdray in Sussex. There I learned many things about our Queen's court, and the sort of men who flock there hoping for favours and advancement." He shook his head. "It is a murky world, of intrigue and danger. As you know, Lady Sarah, your father is one of the wealthiest men in Surrey... But there are those who might wish to see him lose all he has!"

Lady Sarah turned pale.

"I can only tell you my suspicions," he added. "If either of you were to repeat what I say, I could lose my place here. Or at worst, I could end up in a ditch with my throat cut."

Ben and Lady Sarah exchanged glances. After a pause, Henry continued: "The Lodovico plate is more than just a valuable family treasure – it has a history. Before it was given to your father, I believe it came over from France, with the Queen of Scots."

That was a shock, to Ben and Lady Sarah. Everyone knew of the plot hatched several years ago by Mary Stuart, the Queen's cousin, to seize the English throne – a plot which luckily was discovered, but cost the Queen of Scots her head. Ben's own father had been among those who went to London to see her beheaded on Tower Hill. The other plotters had all been executed in the same way. Queen Elizabeth dealt very harshly indeed with traitors.

"If it *is* the same plate," Henry went on, with an excited look in his eyes, "then I think it has an inscription concealed upon it somewhere – in the tracery, or in the settings for the gemstones; I know not where. But I believe that inscription may be the reason why it was taken."

Ben looked stunned. "It must be very important, then," he said, to which Henry nodded fiercely.

"Very likely! It could be a message of some sort – a highly secret one that our own Queen was never meant to see. It might even give the names of people who would have helped the Queen of Scots when she made her bid for power." He sighed. "Your company, Master Ben, merely happened to come along at the right time – or the wrong time, if you like. Whoever wanted to remove the plate could simply blame the theft upon the visiting players!"

"Yes – Gabriel was right," Ben said sadly. "Some think of us as little better than criminals."

"And who would take the word of a criminal," Henry asked, "against a gentleman steward like Thomas Bullen?" He gave a little snort. "Even though he is no true gentleman, in fact..."

He broke off and gazed at Lady Sarah, who was looking very anxious. "Please, Master Henry," she said. "I know you have suspicions – speak them now!"

Henry lowered his eyes. "I have no proof," he said, "but if anyone here is capable of arranging to have the plate stolen, it's Thomas Bullen. I should have guessed sooner," he muttered. "I should have gone to Sir James and told him my theory about the plate – and of my fears that someone else might have learned of it." He turned suddenly to Sarah. "I still should! Isn't that the best course – that we put the whole matter before your father?"

"No!" Lady Sarah cried, making both Henry and Ben jump. "He won't listen... He won't hear a word against Bullen. He trusts him – as he does Lady Anne and her relatives. He thinks I'm just being spiteful whenever I try to tell him otherwise."

She drew a deep breath, and faced Henry. "Please promise me you won't tell him – at least, not yet."

Henry gave a slow nod. "I will wait," he said. "Meanwhile I'll puzzle away at the matter, until I have unravelled it further!"

Lady Sarah looked relieved. "Our best – perhaps our only course, is to find the plate and prove who really stole it. Then you can tell my father about the inscription."

"In theory," Henry replied. "But in practice, I fear it won't be so easy. Especially now the constable arrives..."

Lady Sarah's face fell. "The Pig – you mean he's already here?"

"I heard he will come sometime today," replied Henry.

"But don't you see?" she cried. "Bullen and The Pig are close – they could be in league! Won't that be the way they get the plate away from Bowford, under everyone's noses?"

Henry stared at her. "I suppose it might."

"Then we've no time to lose," she said firmly, and turned to Ben. "We'll start our own search of the house and grounds, this minute."

Ben opened his mouth, then closed it again. He thought it wise not to try and argue with Lady Sarah once she had made up her mind. But Henry looked anxious. "How can you do that, in full view of the household?" he asked.

But Lady Sarah was already moving towards the door. "Come on," she said to Ben. "We've got things to do."

"Wait a minute," Henry cried. "I'm supposed to be teaching you Latin grammar!"

"Sorry," she called back. "Lessons are over for today!"

Ben shrugged, made a quick bow to Henry, and hurried after her. Everything, it seemed, now depended on he and Lady Sarah finding the Lodovico plate.

But what if they couldn't?

Chapter Six

*B*en followed Lady Sarah downstairs, along a passageway and into the great hall.

As they entered the vast hall with its high ceiling, he thought of the performance the company had given two nights ago, of *The Massacre at Paris*. But now he stopped in surprise, for the room looked very different. The long tables which had groaned with food and drink were gone. Only a few chairs remained, round the walls. The hanging curtain at the far end from behind which Lord Bonner's Men had made their entrance had been taken down.

"Come on." Lady Sarah was walking across the floor, which had been spread with clean rushes. Her shoes made swishing sounds.

"But where can we start?" Ben asked, catching up with her at last. "The room's all but empty..."

"The plate was there, on the high table," Lady Sarah said, standing near the wall and pointing. "Imagine it. Now if you were Bullen, and you wanted to steal it, what would you do?"

Ben thought for a moment. "Bribe one of the servants to take it, while they were clearing away?"

Lady Sarah looked unhappy. "I suppose that's the likeliest way, though we've always trusted all our servants... It's horrible to think one of them could be a thief." She took a deep breath. "Very well – imagine the servants clearing away after everyone's gone. If you were the one who wanted to steal the plate, what would you do?"

"I'd make sure no one was watching," Ben answered, "then I'd pile a load of leftovers onto it, and carry it out as if it were an ordinary plate."

"Good!" Lady Sarah nodded. "So the first place we look is the kitchens." She pointed to two doors set in the wall, to either side of where the high table had stood. "One door's for carrying food in," she told Ben. "The other's for carrying it out, so the servingmen don't collide with each other."

"I know that," Ben muttered. He was growing a little tired of Lady Sarah's manner, even though he knew she was trying to help him. But Lady Sarah hadn't noticed, and was already walking out through the door.

There were a lot of people at work in the kitchen. A sweating boy stood by the huge fireplace where a joint of mutton was roasting on a spit, turning it slowly. Servants and kitchen maids were chopping vegetables and mixing things in bowls. One was kneading a big lump of dough to make bread.

As Lady Sarah entered there was a stir, and people stopped to bow and curtsey. Master Lamb the cook, who was tasting something from a dish, looked up in surprise. "My Lady...?"

"Please go on with your duties," Lady Sarah said. "Ben and...my servant and I will not trouble you."

Ben saw several pairs of eyes turn upon him. He was feeling more and more uncomfortable. He spoke under his breath to Lady Sarah. "We can't search here, in front of everyone."

"We have to start somewhere," she retorted.

Ben glanced round the big room, past the corner table where he and the other players took their meals. The back door was open, and led to the kitchen garden. In the distance he could see the brewhouse, and his heart sank to think of poor Solomon imprisoned there, awaiting his fate. Then he noticed Lady Sarah staring at rows of shelves stacked with platters and dishes, as if she expected to see the Lodovico plate sitting amongst them.

"If it was here, it's probably gone now," he said quietly. "Whoever took it could have slipped out the back and given it to someone else…"

"It was the middle of the night!" Lady Sarah hissed back at him. "Anyone outside would need a lantern, and they'd have been seen…"

"All right, then perhaps they simply hid it somewhere close by, then moved it as soon as daylight broke," Ben argued. The search was beginning to look like a hopeless task. He was worried for Solomon, and uncomfortable here with people looking oddly at him. He would rather have faced a huge audience, from the safety of a stage.

"Let's say you're right," Lady Sarah replied. "Then we'll follow the plate out of the door, and see where that takes us."

Ben was relieved to leave the kitchen and get outside. They passed through the doorway and into the garden. Lady Sarah glanced at the brewhouse, then saw Ben's expression. "I know how you must be feeling," she said in a gentler voice. "But this is the only way I can think of to help your friend."

Taking a breath of sweet morning air, Ben glanced about. There was a row of outhouses nearby. Just then a washerwoman came out of one of them carrying a huge basket. The woman saw Lady Sarah, and drew a sharp breath.

"My Lady – there you are! Don't you know the mistress is looking for you?" The woman put down the basket and bobbed a quick curtsey. "You weren't at your lesson with Master Henry."

"I had other things to do, Nan," Lady Sarah answered.

Nan looked at her and smiled. "I know you and your 'other things to do'," she said. "Climbing trees and suchlike, so you end up looking like a ragamuffin." She sighed, then seemed to notice Ben for the first time. "Is this the player boy?"

Ben bowed to her. "Ben Button, mistress."

Lady Sarah spoke up quickly. "May I ask a service of you, Nan?" When Nan nodded, she went on: "Suppose you went back into the wash house for a moment, then came out again and we weren't here. It'd be as if you never saw us at all, wouldn't it? So you couldn't tell me Lady Anne was looking for me..."

Nan hesitated, then saw the look in Lady Sarah's eye, and shook her head slowly. "You'll get me into serious trouble one day, My Lady," she said. Then with a wry look, she picked up her basket and went back into the wash house.

Lady Sarah turned to Ben. "Come on!" she said. And the two of them broke into a run, skirted the edge of the garden and hurried through the archway into the stables – where they stopped dead. For the stable yard was filled with activity.

A large, portly man was dismounting his horse. He handed the reins to one of the grooms who stood by, then stepped down onto the cobbles. And immediately his eyes fell on Lady Sarah.

"My Lady..." He made a stiff bow, which Ben saw was to mock her. His little eyes squinted at her from a fat, fleshy face above a thick brown beard. At once Ben knew this was William Piggott, the constable. He saw why Lady Sarah had named him The Pig.

"Master Piggott." Lady Sarah swallowed, looking uncomfortable. "You're early..."

The Pig was dusting off his cloak and breeches, as if he had endured a long ride instead of just the mile or two from Cobham. He yawned and turned his gaze upon Ben, who stiffened, feeling the constable's eyes boring into him like daggers.

"You, boy," The Pig said. "Fetch me a mug of something – my throat's dry as dust!"

Ben opened his mouth, then saw the look on Lady Sarah's face, and realized that he must act as any servant of hers would. So he bowed and turned to go. The Pig called after him. "Bring two – one for my man Nat."

Now Ben saw another man getting down from his horse, with some difficulty. He was so squat and round-shouldered, he resembled a beetle – especially as his clothing was all black: from the riding cap, down to the fustian breeches and heavy boots. As Nat glanced round, Ben felt as if a cold hand had touched his heart. For he saw in the fellow's gaze, that this was a hard, cruel man. He turned away, and hurried back towards the kitchens.

But now events took a different turn. As Ben left the stable yard he saw two older boys standing on the pathway near the house. One was a servant of some kind; the other was Lady Anne's son, Master Giles.

Ben was unsure whether to hurry on or not. But the matter was soon settled, for Giles was striding towards him. "You, rogue!" he cried as he drew close. "What are you doing outdoors? You dare to flout my father's orders?"

Ben made a quick bow. "I'm here as servant to

Lady Sarah," he began, but the other boy cut him short.

"My sister has no servant, save a simpering lady's maid to dress her. You're looking for things to steal, more like!"

Ben flushed, but stood his ground. He glanced at the servant, and saw that this boy carried a fine peregrine falcon on his wrist. The bird was hooded, and sat quietly upon the thick gauntlet the boy wore.

"Your pardon, sir," Ben said, facing Giles. "But Sir James has ordered me to serve as Lady Sarah's page while I remain here." Then, before he could stop himself, he added: "I thought Lady Sarah was your stepsister, not your sister..."

Giles's face suddenly reddened with anger. "How dare you speak to me in such fashion!" he cried. "I could have you flogged!"

Ben did not answer. He felt surprisingly calm as he waited for Giles to continue. But when he did, it wasn't as Ben expected.

"Come with me, now – I order you!"

Ben hesitated, whereupon Giles grabbed his arm and shoved him. "My falconer and I are going into the woods – you can be our retriever."

Before Ben could reply, the other boy, who looked rather uncomfortable, moved close. "Best to do as you're told," he murmured. And almost before he knew it, Ben was being marched between the two of them, through the kitchen gardens, past the brewhouse and into the wood beyond.

The wood was thick with summer foliage, and the three of them were soon out of sight of the house. Birds of many kinds called out as they walked in silence through the trees. After a while Ben heard the tinkling of water, and saw the ground ahead of them slope down to a clear stream, a few yards wide. Here they stopped, and Giles turned to his servant.

"Loose her here, by the brook," he ordered.

The young falconer looked uneasy. "The trees are too thick, master," he replied. "Best if we crossed the stream and moved uphill, where she can fly more freely..."

But Giles threw him a haughty look. "Do as I say!"

So the boy untied the bird from its leash. It perked up and shook itself as he drew off the hood and raised his arm with a smooth, bowling motion. At once the young falcon spread its wings, lifted its speckled body and flew upwards. They watched it fly off into a tall beech tree, where it landed, folded its wings and sat staring down at them.

Giles muttered under his breath. The falconer said nothing, but Ben could see that the boy knew his job, and had been right. The bird did not want to hunt in the woods, and would probably stay up in the tree for a long time.

"Go and call her down," Giles ordered. "If she won't come you'll have to climb up and get her."

Ben saw the look on the falconer's face, and knew at once that he disliked Giles and his ways as much as Ben did. But the boy had no choice other than to take his order and walk off through the trees.

As soon as he had gone, Giles turned upon Ben with a fury that caught him completely off guard. His fist shot out, cracking Ben on the mouth and sending him reeling. As Ben fought the dizziness that came over him, he saw Giles lunge at him again, and managed to dodge. The blow went wide, but Ben lost his balance and fell forward onto his hands and knees.

Giles stood over him, red-faced and glaring. Sweat was running down his face onto the collar of his fine shirt. As Ben tried to get up, Giles pushed him back down onto his knees again.

"I said you were to be my retriever!" Giles said, his mouth forming a sneer. "So stay down there and bark, until I tell you to rise!"

Ben was breathing steadily, trying not to lose his temper. He knew well enough what would happen if someone of his station dared to raise a hand against one of the nobility. A flogging would only be the start: after that, he could even be sent to prison. He raised his head, and looked Giles in the eye.

"You may do as you like, sir," he said. "But I'm not a dog, and I cannot bark."

"You mean you won't!" Giles cried. "You're a player, aren't you? You can act any part – even a dog. So bark!"

Ben stayed where he was, but made no sound.

"I said bark!" Giles shouted. Then when Ben still remained silent he reached down, grabbed him by the front of his doublet and pulled him roughly to his feet.

"You dare to defy me?" Giles breathed, pushing his face close to Ben's. "I'm the future master of Bowford Manor – I could hire a dozen like you, and have the whole pack of you bark if I wanted to!"

The wood had gone silent. The birds had stopped singing, as if they were watching the events on the ground below. Ben glanced up at Giles, who stood several inches taller than he, and looked over his shoulder to the stream behind. Then unable to stop himself, he shoved Giles in the chest with both hands and watched him stagger backwards, falling with a loud splash into the water.

The next moment seemed like an eternity, though it was only seconds. Yelling and spluttering, Giles got to his feet and stood up to his knees in the shallow stream. Water dripped from his dark hair and ran from his clothes. And it was Giles who now resembled a dog, as he shook himself and scrambled up the bank onto dry ground.

"You...!" Giles spat water from his mouth and stepped forward. "I'll...I'll have you beaten, you..." He stood in his drenched clothes, fists clenched at his sides, almost speechless with rage. But as he raised his hand and started towards Ben, there came a shout from some yards away.

Giles stopped himself and looked round, to see the young falconer walking up behind him. The falcon was already back on his wrist, hooded and leashed.

"You saw him!" Giles shouted, pointing a finger at Ben. "You saw how he shoved me into the brook – I could have been hurt! I'll lay the whole matter before Sir James, and you're my witness!"

There was a brief silence, before the boy spoke. "Your pardon, master," he said quietly. "But I was busy getting the bird down... It seemed to me you lost your footing and fell into the water. The bank's somewhat slippery here."

Ben's heart was thudding. He stared at the boy,

who was looking Giles in the eye, while gently stroking the falcon's wing feathers. Ben guessed that this was to soothe her after her little adventure.

The colour drained from Giles's face, until he was white as a sheet. "What did you say?" he asked in a voice of amazement.

"I saw nothing, Master Giles," the boy answered. "You were already in the water when I came up."

Giles was panting as if he had run a race. He stared at the falconer for what seemed like a long time. Then he shivered from head to foot.

"You should go to the house, sir," the falconer said, "and get out of those wet clothes quick. You could catch a chill, or even a fever."

Still Giles said nothing. Then with a look of fury, he turned and strode off in the direction of the house. But as he went he threw a glance over his shoulder at both of them, which spoke clearly enough.

Ben knew he had not heard the last of the matter; and for the first time, he thought of the consequences of what he had done. Not only he, but all the company could be punished for it. His heart sank.

The falconer gazed at him, and Ben managed a weak smile. "Thank you," he said.

The boy shrugged. "What for? I only told what I saw."

Ben shook his head. "I think you saw what really happened," he answered. "And I don't want you to get into trouble on my account. I'm in enough for two people already."

The falconer said nothing, and the two of them began to head back through the wood. Ben noticed that the boy carried the bird close to his chest.

"Does she have a name?" he asked.

"Master Giles has a fancy name for her, taken from a book," the boy answered. "But I call her Joan. I raised her from an eyass – that's a falcon chick." He looked sideways at Ben. "I'm Edward Stiles – they call me Ned. I'm prentice to Sir James's falconer."

"And I'm Ben Button," Ben told him. "I'm prentice to the players."

Ned Stiles nodded. "I know – your company are the talk of the manor."

By now they had reached the edge of the wood. Ahead was the kitchen garden, and between it and them was the brewhouse. Ben had a sudden urge to see Solomon. He stopped.

"I'll say farewell, if you don't mind," he said. "There's something I have to do."

Ned glanced at him, then at the brewhouse. "If it's your friend you wanted to see," he said, "I think you're too late."

"What do you mean?" Ben began, then gasped: for he now saw that the door to the brewhouse was open. Breaking into a run, he covered the short distance to the building, reached the doorway and stepped inside. The place was empty, save for some barrels and the smell of hops and stale beer. The chain which had bound Solomon to the wall was lying on the floor, but there was no sign of the prisoner.

"How did you know?" he asked, as Ned Stiles came up beside him.

"I heard the constable was going to question all of your company as soon as he arrived," the boy said. "I suppose they've taken the poor fellow up to the house."

After a glance at Ned, Ben hurried off through the kitchen garden towards the big house. As he entered, he heard voices, but didn't stop until he had climbed the stairs and reached the chamber where the players lodged. Throwing open the door, he burst into the room – and found it empty.

Chapter Seven

Ben stood in the chamber, feeling helpless. Then he saw the clothes and baggage lying about – so at least the others hadn't gone far. But remembering the arrival of The Pig, his heart gave a jolt: could they have been taken away for questioning, along with Solomon? He turned to go and came face-to-face with a burly manservant – one of those who had taken Solomon, two nights ago.

"Here you are, boy," the man grunted. "We thought you'd given us all the slip."

"I was looking for my friends—" Ben began.

"They've been brought before the master – and you're to join them," the other replied, jerking his thumb towards the door.

With a heavy heart, Ben followed him out.

A short time later he was ushered into a small room at the rear of the great hall. To his relief the rest of Lord Bonner's men – except Solomon – were seated there on benches. They all looked up as Ben came in.

"You've given us quite a fright, you little rabbit!" Will Sanders was on his feet, but he grunted in surprise as Ben came forward and hugged him tightly.

Will took hold of Ben's shoulders. "What's that bruise on your lip?" he asked. "They haven't hurt you, have they?"

"It's nothing," Ben said. He had never been so glad to see the players in his life. They gathered round him.

"Where have you been?" John asked.

After looking around to make sure no one could overhear, Ben told his tale, about Lady Sarah, Henry Godfrey and the Lodovico plate, and about his tussle with Giles. By the time he had finished the others were seated again, looking as glum as when he had come in.

"I don't like it," Hugh said. "We're being used, like pawns in some chess game..." He turned to Ben.

"This tutor, Godfrey – he says he'll help?"

"If the plate can be found he'll tell Sir James what he suspects," Ben told him, "and we should be cleared of blame – I mean, Solomon should..." He broke off. "Where is Sol?"

"We don't know," Gabriel told him, getting restlessly to his feet. "If you hadn't told us otherwise, I'd have thought he was still locked up in that brewhouse."

Will was frowning. "That Giles needs watching," he said. "A nasty piece of work..." He stopped as the door opened, and a silence fell. For in the doorway was the steward, Thomas Bullen. And once again, he was wearing his cold smile. His gaze soon turned upon Ben, who feared the worst. Ben was sure that by now Giles must have told his mother, and perhaps Sir James too, of what had happened in the wood. He swallowed, awaiting his fate.

But Bullen's eyes switched to the others. "Now you're all here, you can come in and thank Sir James for his mercy," he said. "Not to mention his hospitality. Many a nobleman would have merely cast you out at the first inkling of trouble."

"What do you mean?" John asked, but Bullen was already turning to go.

"Follow me," he said, "and mind your manners."

Two men in Bowford livery, with daggers at their belts, appeared outside, eyeing the players grimly. Without a word the five of them walked into the great hall, with the guards close behind.

The players lined up before a long table in the middle of the hall. The Pig stood behind the table, staring at them all with his greedy little eyes. To Ben's dismay, Giles sat beside him. He must have changed his clothes quickly, since the ducking he had received earlier. Giles ignored the other players, but looked hard at Ben.

Sir James looked at John Symes, and his first words took them all by surprise. "You are free to leave here," he said. "Indeed, I think it's best you pack up and go before midday. Then you will have enough daylight to travel by."

"But what of Solomon – Master Tree—" John began.

"The prisoner is being taken for questioning."

It was Bullen who spoke. He waved a hand towards The Pig, who was helping himself to more wine. Seeing everyone watching, the constable straightened up quickly.

"Master Piggott the constable has custody," Bullen said. "He will investigate, and if he's satisfied of the man's guilt, he will take the proper action."

The players looked at each other anxiously, then at The Pig. "I'm the law in this parish," he announced. "The thief is on his way to Cobham, to be held in my lock-up. The matter's no longer your concern. And I warn you..." He glared at them. "We want no vagabonds there. It's a respectable village, so I'd advise you to move on, and quick!"

At once Ben realized what had happened: The Pig's assistant, the evil-looking Nat, had already taken Solomon away. What that might mean, he did not like to imagine.

Hugh Cotton was about to speak, but at a glance from John Symes he dropped his gaze. There seemed no point in protesting. Without a word, they turned to go. But then came a harsh voice, which stopped them dead.

"The boy should stay behind – for he is also a thief!"

There was a sudden stir. Watched by everyone, Giles got to his feet, pointing a finger at Ben. "I encountered him a short while ago, skulking about in the gardens," he told Sir James. "Soon after, I found that my dagger was missing. I must have dropped it, so I went back to look, but there was no sign. I say the players' chamber should be searched!"

Sir James frowned at Ben. "What have you to say to that?" he asked.

Ben's mouth was dry. He tried to remain calm. "I'm no thief, sir," he said. "And I know nothing of any dagger."

John Symes looked straight at Sir James. "This is another grave mistake!" he cried. "The boy is my prentice, who lives in my own house. He's honest and true—"

"Be silent!" Thomas Bullen had risen. "Let the chamber be searched at once," he said to Sir James. "I will accompany the constable. If nothing's found, they can all be on their way."

There was a tense moment, before the master of Bowford sighed and nodded. "Very well," he said.

Briskly the steward strode towards the door. The Pig banged his cup down and followed. Last came the players, ushered out by stony-faced men-at-arms.

But even before they climbed the stairs to their chamber, Ben knew what was about to happen. He had a sick feeling in his stomach, for he guessed what Giles had done. Soon he was standing with the rest of the company at one side of the room, watching the Bowford guards ransack their belongings.

Impatiently, The Pig looked round at Ben. "Which pack is yours?" he demanded.

Ben's pack lay beside his pallet, which was the smallest. In silence, he pointed to it. It was no surprise to him when one of the guards opened it, and with a cry pulled out a silver-hilted dagger.

John gripped Ben's shoulder to show that he knew what had happened, before Ben was seized and taken outside.

Chapter Eight

The next few hours were the unhappiest Ben had known in years – in fact, since the day his father had died.

At first he was marched back to the great hall. But instead of being handed over to The Pig as he feared, Ben was told he would remain at Bowford Manor while Sir James decided what to do. His one ray of hope was that Sir James did not seem convinced by the sudden appearance of the dagger in Ben's baggage. But before he could plead his innocence again, he was ushered out and taken to the kitchens.

A short while later he was standing before the cook, Master Lamb, who looked him up and down. "You're to remain in my keeping for the present," he said. "Do you know anything about kitchen work?"

Ben shook his head. The kitchen servants were all staring at him. He had never felt so alone in his life.

"You'll sleep there," the cook said, pointing to an empty corner. "When you've time to sleep that is. There aren't enough hours in the day to do all that we have to do."

A blonde-haired girl came in the back door carrying a heavy pail, and Master Lamb called to her. "Jane! This boy's in your charge – keep him busy." And without further word he stalked off.

Jane was about sixteen years old. She wore a greasy smock, and her hands were red from scrubbing. She pointed to a pile of dishes on a nearby table. "You'd best bring those," she said, and walked outside.

There was a big tub full of water in the yard, and Ben was set to work washing things. In fact for the rest of that long day, he did nothing else. Every time he thought he had finished, another pile of pots and platters would arrive. By late afternoon his back was aching, and he thought he must have washed up every dish in the house.

At last, Jane came to tell him he could stop and have supper. Painfully he straightened up and went inside, to the same table where, only that morning, he had taken a breakfast of porridge with the rest of Lord Bonner's men. Now, he felt as if he would never see them again. But surely, he thought, John wouldn't desert him? Unhappily he sat down at the table.

The other kitchen servants took no notice of Ben, but talked among themselves. There was a trencher before him and a knife, and he was so hungry that he grabbed a hunk of bread and some cheese, and stuffed them into his mouth. There was plenty of food, though it was mainly leftovers from whatever Sir James, his family and their higher servants had eaten that day, or the day before. There was even the remains of a huge carp. Ben took some of the fish, and found it good. He was still munching when Jane tapped him on the shoulder and pointed towards the back door, which always seemed to be open. He was surprised to see Ned Stiles, the young falconer, standing in the doorway, holding a bunch of game birds tied together with twine.

"Go and take the partridges off him," Jane said. "We'll pluck them later."

Ben rose and went to the door, but as he drew

close, Ned bent and whispered in his ear. "I've a message for you. Come outside after sunset."

Then he handed him the birds, and left.

Ben could hardly wait for the sun to set. When it did, work at last stopped for the day. Pallets and blankets were spread on the floor for the male servants. The women, including Jane, went off to another part of the house. Ben asked if he could get some air before bed, and was told he could, so long as he did not leave the kitchen garden.

He stood outside in the cool of the evening and looked around, whereupon a voice startled him.

"Over here!"

He looked to his right, but saw no one, so he followed the sound, past the outbuildings until he stood under a tree by a fence. And now a figure appeared out of the dusk.

"Ned..." Ben stepped forward, but the young falconer spoke quickly.

"I've only a minute, before my master wonders where I am," he said.

"You said you had a message." As his eyes grew accustomed to the dim light, Ben saw that Ned was fumbling in his jerkin. He brought out a folded piece of paper and handed it to him.

"Can you read?" he asked.

"Yes, there's a school in my village," Ben told him.

"Well, I've two messages," Ned said. "This is from Lady Sarah. Swear you will not say I gave it you, or we'll both be in trouble."

"I swear," Ben said, taking the paper with some excitement. "Where's the other one?"

"That's by mouth," Ned answered. "I saw your friends, the other players, leave at midday. I helped them load the cart."

Ben's eyes widened, as Ned went on: "Master Symes said to tell you they would make straight for Oatlands. It's but five miles away, down in the Thames Valley."

"Oatlands?" Ben muttered, then remembered. "Isn't that one of the Queen's palaces?"

"Yes. He said to tell you they would seek help there, and get word to His Lordship – Lord Bonner, isn't it? Then they'll be back for you, as soon as they can. He said to keep your chin up, and trust him."

"I knew he wouldn't desert me!" Ben exclaimed.

Ned glanced towards the house. "Mayhap I shouldn't tell you this, but I also saw the constable's man take your other friend away. He was tied on a long rope, walking behind his horse."

"Poor Solomon!" Ben cried in dismay. "What will they do to him?"

Ned shrugged, but made no reply.

"I must do something," Ben cried, clenching his fists. He thought desperately of Lady Sarah, and her plan to find the plate. He had seen nothing of her since the morning. And now Solomon had been hauled away, like a criminal...

"I can't stay here," he said unhappily. "Perhaps I should run away to Oatlands and find the others – I could go tonight!"

But Ned put out a hand and gripped Ben's arm. "Think!" he said urgently. "Wouldn't that make you look like a thief? And anyway, how would you find your way in the dark? You don't know the roads... They would go after you on horseback and hunt you down in no time."

Ben lowered his gaze, looking miserable. "I suppose you're right," he admitted.

"Read Lady Sarah's message before you do anything," Ned told him. "Now, I must go."

"Again, I should thank you," Ben said. "You've been a true friend."

Ned sighed. "I know what Master Giles is like," he said. "And I don't think you are a thief." And quickly, he disappeared in the gathering dark.

Slowly, Ben walked back to the kitchens, with Lady Sarah's letter still in his hand. He reached the door, and peered in to see the servants preparing their beds. The light of several candles spilled out of the doorway, but he knew they would soon be extinguished. He had one chance to look at the letter before he went to bed. Quickly he unfolded it, and read.

To Master Ben Button:
I am disciplined by Lady Anne for skipping my lessons, and confined to my chamber. So I cannot help you look for the Lodovico plate. They will not let you be my page any more, nor am I allowed to speak to you. But Master Henry is still our friend and does not believe you a thief, nor do I. Ned the falconer's boy might be of service. You must find the plate quickly, or Henry thinks it will be too late. Without the plate he cannot prove who really stole it, and so expose any treachery on the part of Bullen, or anyone else.

One day, if I ever become mistress of Bowford, I will reward you handsomely. And I know you are not a coward.

Given under my hand this day,
Lady Sarah Howard.

Voices sounded from the kitchen, and someone moved towards the door. Quickly Ben folded the letter and stuffed it inside his shirt. He walked in, to see the cook holding a candle and staring at him. "Had enough exercise now?" he asked.

Ben nodded, and went towards his pallet.

In the night Ben awoke, hearing a barn owl calling from the wood. At once he remembered the joke he had played by the roadside in Southwark, when gloomy Solomon had said that their journey was doomed. His eyes filled with tears. How this was all going to end, he had no idea.

In the morning after breakfast, Ben helped Jane pluck the partridges Ned had brought in the day before. They sat outside in the sunshine, while gardeners went about their business, wheeling barrows, hoeing and weeding. Seeing how quiet he was, Jane tapped him on the arm.

"Cheer up, player boy. Worse things could happen."

"Like what?" Ben asked her. He was restless, wishing he could be elsewhere: searching for the Lodovico plate so that he could save Solomon. How he might do that while he was confined to the kitchen yard, he couldn't imagine.

"Like what?" Jane sniffed. "You think this is hard work? You should see what it's like when the master and mistress have a banquet, like that night you gave your show. We've that much to do, we haven't time to draw breath!"

"You mean our coming here just made more work for you?" Ben asked.

Jane shook her head. "They'd have entertained in any case. Nobles like Sir James have to do it, to show how important they are. It's expected." She stopped pulling feathers, and smiled to herself. "The Queen herself came here once," she said. "A year or so back...you should have seen the procession of folk she brought with her. Like an army it was! And all dressed in such finery...silks and jewels..." Her smile faded, to be replaced by a bitter look. "Would that I could afford such things! But then..." She gazed into the distance, and said to herself: "Maybe one day, I will!"

Ben was thinking fast, wondering what he might discover. He decided to be bold. "Can I ask you something?"

"What is it?" Jane asked suspiciously.

"Do you truly believe one of our company stole that golden plate?"

Her eyes widened. "You think one of the household would do such a thing?"

"No – I mean, of course not," Ben said quickly. "Only—"

"You little rogue!" Jane's face flushed to the roots of her blonde hair. "We're decent folk, and loyal to Sir James – every one of us!"

"I know," Ben said, wishing he had never opened his mouth. "It's just that I know Solomon, and he wouldn't do such a thing either..."

But Jane was scowling. "Enough!" she cried. "You should think yourself lucky to be put to honest work like this, instead of being taken to jail like the other one. Now hurry up and get these finished!" With that she got to her feet, and was about to walk away when she stopped, glancing towards the wash house.

"And don't you go bothering Nan!" she told Ben. "She's my friend, and she's got enough to do without you getting under her feet!" Then she stalked off into the kitchen.

Feeling utterly unhappy, Ben bent to his task of pulling feathers. But a short time later Jane reappeared and told him to stop; for he was called to the morning room, to stand before Sir James and hear his judgement.

Chapter Nine

Trying not to show how scared he was, Ben faced Sir James across the table. To his relief the master of Bowford was alone, apart from a few servants who stood in attendance. Sir James lowered what appeared to be a letter, and looked squarely at Ben.

"Your fellows think very highly of you," he said.

"Thank you, sir," was all Ben could manage.

"They have written to me," Sir James went on, "with a copy of a letter they've sent to your patron, Lord Bonner. It seems His Lordship will join the

Queen at Oatlands in a few days. Her Majesty sometimes goes there on her summer progresses."

Ben wondered where this was leading: Sir James seemed uneasy. "You still claim you don't know how Master Giles's dagger got into your pack?" he asked suddenly.

Ben nodded. "I swear it, sir."

Sir James got to his feet and strolled over to the window, then turned to Ben.

"I will not send you to the constable," he said.

Ben sighed with relief.

"However," Sir James added, "even though the dagger was recovered, I am not satisfied. There's bad blood between you and my stepson which will not be tolerated. Were it not for the protection of your patron, you would have been flogged."

Ben was silent. He knew that the company's patron, Lord Bonner, was an important man – higher in rank than a knight like Sir James. Sir James would not wish to offend him by punishing one of his players without good reason.

"I will give you a choice. You may join your fellows at Oatlands, where they await the arrival of Lord Bonner. Or..."

Ben's heart leaped with joy, but he managed to hide it, for Sir James had not finished.

"Or," he went on, "you can remain here until I am able to speak with His Lordship. We'll find work for you, and you will have a bed and full board while…" He frowned. "While matters are investigated further."

At that, Ben's heart sank. He thought of poor Solomon, locked up in Cobham. And he thought of Lady Sarah, and of the Lodovico plate, and how important it was that he find it. Now she was confined to her room, there was no one else to search… He swallowed and took a deep breath, for he knew what he must do.

"I will stay in your service for the present, sir," he said.

The servants looked at him in surprise. So did Sir James. "Then you may return to the kitchens," he said. "Work hard and conduct yourself well, and I'll take it into account when I meet with His Lordship."

And that was the end of it. Ben bowed, and was taken through the long stone passages, back to the heat of the kitchen.

But to his surprise, after that there was a marked difference in the way he was treated. Word seemed to get round Bowford Manor of what he had said, when Sir James offered him the choice of leaving. If he was truly a thief, people seemed to think, he would have gone away the first chance he got. So perhaps he was an honest lad, after all...

As for Ben, though his heart was heavy at being separated from the other players, he felt that he had done the right thing. Though how he was supposed to find the Lodovico plate by himself, he did not know.

That afternoon he was given a basket of dirty linen and told to take it out to Nan Fowler the washerwoman. The order made him uneasy, mindful as he was of what Jane had told him. But struggling with the heavy basket, he walked towards the wash house and found Nan outside, spreading bed sheets on the bushes to dry. When she saw Ben, she stopped and stared.

"You've become the talk of Bowford, young man," she said. "Do you know that?"

Ben blushed and put down the basket. To his surprise, Nan stepped closer and lowered her voice.

"Did you read Lady Sarah's letter?"

He drew a breath, but said nothing.

"Don't fret yourself," Nan said. "Who do you think it was smuggled it out of the house, and passed it to Ned Stiles?"

Ben stared. "You?"

"I'm Lady Sarah's friend," Nan said. "I promised her mother before she died I'd always look out for her." She gazed down at Ben. "Well – did you read it or not?" When Ben nodded, she asked: "What did it say?"

When he had finished telling her, Nan glanced around. Gardeners were working some distance away. Quickly she picked up the basket. "In here," she said, and led the way into the wash house.

The interior was warm and damp, and smelled of lye soap and dirty washing. Baskets lay around full of clothes and bedding. There was a huge buck tub standing on blocks, brimming with frothy water. Nan peered into it, then picked up a long stick and began poking at the contents.

"By the heavens, Master Ben," she said. "You're caught up in quite a little adventure, aren't you? This missing plate must be very valuable..." She jabbed hard at the washing with her stick. "Well now – let's think how we can help you in your search."

Ben watched her stir the soaking clothes. He felt encouraged: perhaps he was not so alone after all. "If only I wasn't stuck in the kitchen," he said to Nan. "Then I could move about the manor..."

Nan thought for a moment. "Master Lamb could

manage without you well enough. The turnspit boy does all the things you do, as a rule... Wait, I have it!" She turned to him. "You ever done any gardening?"

Ben blinked. "I used to help my mother in the garden back home in Hornsey. That's the village I come from."

"That'll do," Nan said. "Then when you're out and about, you can search where you like. So long as no one sees you."

Ben was starting to get excited. Not only could he look around, he might see Ned Stiles...perhaps he could even get messages to Lady Sarah. Then his face fell.

"Would Sir James allow it?" he asked. "I know the steward won't...he thinks I'm a rogue."

"Never mind him," Nan replied. "I'll speak to Master Lamb for you, and he'll ask Sir James. He holds a special place here, being the best cook in Surrey." She smiled. "I'll ask him tonight after supper. No time like the present, is there?"

Ben smiled back.

And that night, when he drifted off to sleep on his pallet in the kitchen, there was still a smile on his face. For he had been told to collect his belongings first thing in the morning and present himself to Tom Beech, the chief gardener.

*

Master Beech was a short man with thick, brawny arms; his skin brown and leathery from being outdoors all the time. He was wearing an old straw hat, and a threadbare smock with the sleeves rolled up. When Ben stood before him outside the big tool house, which the gardeners used as a kind of headquarters, Beech gazed down at him, sighed and shook his head.

"Snakes and lizards, boy – ye've no muscles on ye! What if there's digging to do?"

"I can pull weeds, sir," Ben said. "And set seeds in rows, and water things from a can..."

"Whoa!" Master Beech held up a hand. "Maytime's as good as over. What little planting there is now, needs a skilled man to it." He squinted into the sun, which was rising above the treetops. Then to Ben's alarm, he doubled up suddenly and gave a huge, bellowing sneeze, the loudest Ben had ever heard in his life.

"Ahhh...that's better!" The gardener straightened up, blowing like a horse. "Can't start the day proper, till I've cleared my pipes..." He frowned at Ben. "What's that you were saying?"

"Nothing, sir," Ben answered. "I'll work hard, whatever duties you wish to give me."

Master Beech sniffed. "That's well said. I dare say I can find a use for you." He pointed to the tool house. "Stow your pack in there. You can sleep inside tonight with the prentices."

Ben did as he was told. When he came out again Master Beech was walking off between raised soil beds, beckoning him to follow. In the far corner of the garden, Ben caught sight of the brewhouse, and shuddered.

"You said you could weed." Beech stopped beside a bed of greens and pointed. "Can you tell which is which?"

"I see the spring cabbages and the kale," Ben answered. "I suppose the rest are weeds…"

"Bullseye!" Beech cleared his throat, and spat on the path. He reminded Ben of the men in the theatres who took tobacco, and were always coughing.

"Start here and work your way to the end," he said. "Throw the weeds in that barrow, and when it's full, take it to the tool house. You'll see the spoil heap, beyond."

Ben bent down to start his work as Master Beech walked off. Glancing towards the big house, Ben saw Jane come out of the kitchen door struggling with a heavy pail. And for the first time in days, he thought himself lucky.

After that, unknown to everyone, Ben began to search the grounds of Bowford Manor for the Lodovico plate. At first he could only look round the garden as he weeded, which soon became a waste of time. Surely whoever had stolen the valuable plate would not have buried it? He shook his head: too risky. One of the gardeners could easily come across it; there were so many of them wandering about.

He tried to think of less obvious places where such an object could have been concealed. The first one that caught his eye was the well, which was not far from the kitchen door. Wheeling his barrow, Ben managed to overturn it nearby; and while he was picking up the weeds, he had a good look down the well. But its stone sides were worn smooth, and the water was a very long way down, so that he could see nothing but darkness. A rope led from a stout beam fixed over the well to the handle of the pail, which was empty. There were no other places a rope could be attached. Try as he might he could not see how the plate, even if it was wrapped up and tied in a bundle, could have been lowered down the well without someone noticing it.

His next thought was the stables nearby, through the archway in the garden wall. And that same afternoon, an opportunity arose to inspect them.

The gardeners, about a dozen of them, were taking their midday dinner of bread and cheese washed down with watered beer. They sat in the shade of the tool house, gossiping and joking, but their country accents were so strong, Ben could hardly understand a word they said. After a while Tom Beech appeared, calling for everyone's attention.

"We need manure from the stable yard," he announced. "'Tis a smelly task in this weather, but someone needs to do it."

Ben stood up. "I'll go," he said.

The other men looked up, and one or two of them laughed. But their master silenced them with a frown. "Good lad," he said. "Fetch it over to yon bed of sweet peas, and I'll give you a farthing for your trouble."

The yard was quiet in the warm afternoon. Flies buzzed about the big heap of horse manure mixed with straw, which lay in a corner. Ben wheeled his barrow over and began forking the mixture into it. As he did so he glanced around, trying to think of places a thief might have hidden the golden plate. But the more he looked, the more disappointed he grew. There was nowhere which would serve such a purpose.

Then he thought of the manure heap, but after prodding around in it with his fork, he found nothing underneath. He was still thinking the matter over, when heavy footsteps sounded on the cobbles behind him. He turned round to find himself facing the groom he and Lady Sarah had confronted three days ago, over the fellow's neglect of Tarlton.

"You again!" The man glared. "What are you doing in my yard?" But he did not want to listen to Ben's answer. "Do what you've been sent to do, and be on your way," he grunted. "And remember I've got my eye on you, in case anything goes missing!"

He walked off, leaving Ben to reflect that not everyone at Bowford now thought well of him. He glanced towards the stable, wondering if Lady Sarah's pony Tamora was inside. Then he picked up the fork, and finished his task.

He wheeled the barrow to the flower bed, and was duly rewarded with a farthing by Master Beech. Despite his gruff ways, Ben liked the head gardener more and more. He wished he could tell him his secret; who would know better where a thief might hide the plate?

Late in the afternoon, when the air had cooled and the shadows grew longer, Master Beech called Ben over.

"You've worked well, boy," he said, "so I'm going to give 'ee a little treat. Come along – and stick close to me."

He gestured Ben to pick up a hoe and follow him. They went out of the kitchen garden, and along the pathway round the side of the manor. Then they stopped at a sight Ben had not yet seen: the splendid formal gardens at the front of the house. Here were lawns, flower beds, marble statues, and hedges cut into the shapes of birds and beasts.

Master Beech stopped by a bed and told Ben to pull the weeds while he inspected the flowers. "Sir James planted these roses for his first wife, Lady Catherine," Beech said. "Lady Sarah's mother..." He became thoughtful for a moment. "A fine lady, she was; always cheerful... Made you feel good just to be there when she was about." He sniffed, then saw Ben watching him, and coughed noisily.

They worked in silence for a while, until Ben heard voices. Glancing up, he saw a group of people in fine clothes coming out of the house. As they strolled onto the lawn he saw who they were, and bent his head quickly to his work.

The first was Sir Ralph Gosson, who was deep in conversation with the steward, Thomas Bullen. Ben could see his bald head shining in the sun.

Behind them walked Master Giles and Lady Anne, accompanied by two or three ladies-in-waiting. Of Sir James, there was no sign.

The group walked slowly between the beds. If they noticed the head gardener and the boy who was helping him, they did not show it. Ben felt uncomfortable, even though he had permission to be here. For some reason he did not want these people to see him – though he would dearly have liked to know what they were talking about; they seemed very serious. He thought of Lady Sarah, and how much she would hate having to remain indoors on such a sunny day. Then he remembered the task he had taken upon himself, of searching for the Lodovico plate, and his spirits fell. Glancing across the gardens, to the paddock and the meadows beyond, he saw then how impossible his task was. The grounds of Bowford were vast, stretching for what seemed like miles. How could anyone search them alone? It would be like looking for a needle in a hundred haystacks. And in any case, it was probably too late. Perhaps the plate was already gone – and Solomon Tree was to be condemned for it.

He must have sighed to himself, for Master Beech called to him from a few yards away. "Weary, boy?

Well this'll cheer ye: tomorrow's the Sabbath day, when we can all rest our bones. How does that strike ye?"

Ben nodded, and managed a smile.

Chapter Ten

The next morning Ben put on his best clothes and followed the other servants to the Bowford chapel for Sunday service.

The chapel was in a wing of the great house, and it was packed to the doors. Ben was in one of the back pews, where the servants were crammed: lady's maids, kitchen wenches and servingmen, gardeners and grooms and all the other folk that made up the large household of an important nobleman like Sir James Howard. Ben saw Ned Stiles, but he was too far away to talk to. He could see Sir James at the front in the family pew, which was made of fine oak and carved with the Howard coat of arms. Lady Anne, Giles and Sir Ralph were also there, along with Thomas Bullen. As he had hoped, there, too, was Lady Sarah.

She was dressed in a black gown and a linen hood, and as Ben watched she moved suddenly, as if she knew someone was looking at her. But when the old, white-haired parson came in to begin his sermon, she bent her head and did not lift it again. Come what may, Ben was determined to speak with her. And when the congregation filed out after the service, he saw his chance.

The nobles left first, in a stately procession, followed by the servants in order of importance. To his impatience, Ben was not allowed out until last, along with the gardener's prentices, two older boys who paid him no attention. As he emerged into the stone-flagged passage outside, he saw Lady Sarah disappearing round a corner. Trying not to think about the trouble he might be getting into, he hurried after her, ducking and dodging his way through. People muttered as he ran, and someone called out, but Ben did not stop until he had rounded the corner into another passage with a staircase. Here at last he caught up with Lady Sarah as she began to climb the steps. Just ahead of her was a figure in black which he now realized was her tutor, Master Henry.

"My Lady!" Ben called, out of breath. He skidded to a halt, and made his bow.

"Ben!" Lady Sarah's face lit up at once. Then she seemed alarmed. "You mustn't talk to me – I'm in disgrace for skipping my lessons..."

"I just wanted you to know that I've been carrying out the plan," Ben said urgently.

"Quiet, you fool!" It was Henry Godfrey who spoke, stumbling down the steps towards Ben. He glanced around. People had gone off to various parts of the house, but there was still a murmur of voices from the main hallway.

"Impulsive boy!" the tutor muttered, though his expression was one of concern rather than anger. "You want to get us all into trouble?"

"Please, Master Henry," Lady Sarah said, unhappily. "This is all my fault..." She faced Ben. "I shouldn't have raised your hopes as I did," she told him. "There's nothing more you can do. The plate is almost certainly gone by now. You should have taken the offer my father made you, and gone to rejoin your company."

Ben gasped. "But Solomon's in jail in Cobham, and—"

"It's too late!" Lady Sarah persisted. "Go and ask to speak with my father – tell him you've changed your mind."

Ben's heart had sunk so low, he thought it would never lift again. "How can I?" he asked. "Who else is there to try and unmask the real thief, and set Solomon free?"

Lady Sarah was about to respond, when suddenly she looked past him and drew breath. At the same time Master Henry let out a groan, and made a low bow.

Even before Ben turned, he knew that his recklessness had not gone unnoticed. He heard footsteps and a swish of heavy skirts, and the next moment was face-to-face with one of the people he dreaded most. He bowed, and hung his head.

"Well, this is a most interesting gathering," Lady Anne said in a voice of ice. "Is anyone going to tell me what it's all about?"

Since neither Lady Sarah nor Ben made a reply, Master Henry slowly cleared his throat. "My Lady, I should take the blame," he began. "I was—"

"You will leave us!" Lady Anne snapped. And her eyes blazed at the tutor, as if she wished to strike him dead.

Henry coughed nervously, started to make another

bow, then thought better of it and hurried away up the stairs.

Now Lady Anne turned furiously upon Lady Sarah. "How dare you flout my instructions!"

Lady Sarah flushed, but stood her ground. "I've done nothing wrong, madam," she answered. "Nor has the boy..."

"The boy," Lady Anne cut in sharply, "is a wretched little sneak-thief." She glanced at Ben as if he were an insect. "He's no right to be here – and he will be punished for it."

Ben stood miserably, wondering whether he was supposed to go away or wait to be dismissed. He decided to wait.

"Well?" Lady Anne stared at Lady Sarah, until she lowered her eyes. "I want to know what you were doing!"

Lady Sarah hesitated, then replied: "I was asking the boy to look in on my pony, and see that she is being well cared for."

Lady Anne gave a snort, a bit like a horse herself. "Why shouldn't she be?" she demanded. "Don't you think the grooms know their tasks well enough?"

"Yes, My Lady." Lady Sarah appeared contrite, but Ben knew that she was acting. He thought her performance not at all bad, for an amateur.

Now Lady Anne turned her icy gaze upon him, and it was all he could do not to flinch. "Return to your duties," she ordered, "and await your punishment."

Ben bowed and turned to go. As he walked off around the corner, he heard Lady Anne say: "Water and rye bread shall be your diet for the rest of the day, you little weasel. Now go to your chamber and stay there until I decide your fate!"

Once outside, Ben walked and walked, neither noticing nor caring where he went. The house and the kitchen garden were soon behind him. Some of the gardeners were about but he paid them no attention, and nobody called to him. Past the brewhouse he trudged, into the wood where he had tangled with Giles three days ago. Soon he heard running water and came upon the brook where Giles had received his soaking. He walked along the bank for a while, found a line of stepping stones in the stream, and crossed over it. Then he was following a rough path through the undergrowth, with the ground rising beneath his feet. The trees thinned out, and he found himself on a broad, grassy hill dotted with wild flowers. There he stopped, sat down and put his chin in his hands. For what seemed a long time he stayed there, feeling small and alone, wondering what on earth he was going to do.

Now, it struck him that there was nothing to stay at Bowford for. And he missed John and Hugh and the rest of Lord Bonner's men so much, he could have wept. It seemed his only course was to ask Sir James if he could go to Oatlands after all. The difficulty was Solomon. Somehow Ben felt it was up to him to prove Solomon's innocence – which meant finding the Lodovico plate. But if Lady Sarah believed it had already left the manor...

He sighed. There was no one else left to help Solomon. And if no one could find out who had really stolen the plate, Sol would be condemned for it – perhaps even hanged. The torments he might already have suffered, Ben did not like to think about. He clenched his fists at the cruel injustice of it all. He wished he had never heard of the famous gold plate, or of Bowford Manor. The company should never have come here. Solomon had been right all along: the journey was doomed from the start.

He stood up, squinting into the morning sun. He would have to find someone to ask Sir James if Ben might speak with him. The only person he could think of was Nan the washerwoman. It looked as if she was the only friend he had.

But he had forgotten someone. As he began to head back and reached the bank of the stream again, there came a shout from the other side. He peered through the trees and saw the young falconer, Ned Stiles, with a hooded bird on his wrist.

At the sight of Ned, Ben's spirits lifted a little. Raising his hand, he quickened his pace and reached the stepping stones. Ned walked towards him and crossed the stream. As he drew close he saw Ben's expression, and stopped. "You look like you've got the whole world on your shoulders," he said. "I'm going to exercise Joan. Why don't you walk with me?"

As they walked, Ben found himself telling Ned his troubles. By the time he reached the end of his tale they were on the hilltop, where Ned unhooded Joan and allowed her to soar up into the sky. Then he turned thoughtfully to Ben.

"If you go to Oatlands," he said, "then at least you'll be with your company again."

"I can't go without seeing Solomon," Ben said unhappily. "I need to know he's all right."

"Then go into Cobham and seek him. Today's Sunday. You're free to do as you wish."

"I can't leave Bowford without permission," Ben replied.

"Well..." Ned smiled suddenly. "Why not go in

disguise? They say you act well. So dress up as a country lad, and I'll go with you." Then a thought struck him: "Even better – you could dress as a girl. That's what you do on the stage, isn't it? I can say you're my cousin!"

"You'd go with me?" Ben stared at him.

"Why not?" Ned shrugged. "It isn't far, and I've time to myself this afternoon. I can show you the way – and I've an idea where they'll be holding your friend."

He peered about, shading his eyes from the sun. Ben followed his gaze and saw Joan gliding out of the trees towards them. Expertly Ned raised his arm and allowed the falcon to land on his gauntlet. He hooded her, then turned to Ben.

"Well, master player. What do you say?"

Ben broke into a smile.

Chapter Eleven

*I*f anyone had been watching that afternoon, they would have seen two young folk walk out of the gates of Bowford Manor and strike westward on the road that led towards Cobham. One was Ned Stiles, the prentice falconer; the other looked like a kitchen maid in drab clothes, perhaps on her way to visit relatives in the village. Together they trudged downhill along the dusty road, and the manor was soon behind them.

The dress Ned had borrowed from his sister reached right down to Ben's feet. Underneath it Ben wore his own plain shoes and hose, and hoped no one would notice them. On his head was a linen cap. He was used to playing girls' roles – but this was different. If this was acting, he thought, it was unlike any he had done before, since there was no plot to work from, and no lines to remember. He would have to trust his instincts as well as his talent. His main worry was that the country accent he was about to attempt would not work. Perhaps it would be best to let Ned Stiles do the talking, if talking were needed.

In a short time Cobham appeared before them. The village was almost encircled by a bend in the River Mole, which sparkled in the distance. Ben saw watermills on the river, and closer to, a church tower. The old timber and thatch houses clustered about the church, and soon the two boys were walking among them.

"Where's the jail?" Ben asked.

"There isn't one," Ned replied.

Ben stopped in his tracks. "What do you mean?"

"You ever known a place this size that had its own lock-up?"

Ben thought of his own small village of Hornsey. The only means of punishment there was the ancient stocks, which were seldom used. His spirits sank. "Then where—"

"Trust me, and keep walking," Ned told him. "The street leads down to the river, and one of the riverside cottages belongs to Piggott. There's an outhouse round the back where he keeps his cider. That's the place to look."

Ben picked up his pace again. The village was almost deserted on this warm Sunday afternoon. Perhaps folk were taking naps, or digging their gardens. The two of them passed an inn with a sign showing a white lion standing on its hind legs. They could hear voices from inside.

"If I know Piggott," Ned muttered, "he'll be in there filling his fat belly." Instinctively Ben pulled his cap lower, and hurried on.

Soon they stood near the riverside, beside a row of small cottages. The end one had a garden with apple trees. Ned nudged Ben and pointed to it. "The constable's house."

The house looked so peaceful and so ordinary, Ben could not imagine someone like The Pig living there. He turned to Ned, but he was already moving round the wattle fence that bordered the garden. Ben followed and saw, as Ned had described, an outbuilding at the back of the house.

"Stay here and keep watch," Ned told him.

Ben stood with his back to the fence, where he

might see anyone approaching. Anxiously he waited while Ned climbed over the fence, crossed the garden and disappeared. But in a few minutes he was back, slightly out of breath.

"What's happened?" Ben asked.

"He's not there," Ned answered. "The lean-to's empty."

"Then where—"

"We can't stay here," Ned interrupted. "Come on."

He led the way back up the street. But as they passed the White Lion Inn again, a squat figure in black clothes reeled out of the doorway, right into their path. Both boys stopped, as they recognized the man: none other than The Pig's servant, the evil-looking Nat.

"Who's this?" The man stood peering at them. Ben could only hope he had not been recognized. He smelled the beer fumes on Nat's breath and saw that he was not only drunk, but dangerous.

Ned Stiles started to move, but Nat sidestepped to block his way. "I know you – you're the falconer's boy from Bowford." Ned nodded, whereupon the fellow swung his gaze upon Ben. "Who're you?"

Ben swallowed. He had been so concerned about his disguise he had forgotten to think of a false name. His mind was blank.

"I'm...Bess Button, sir," he blurted out.

At once he regretted using his own surname. He hoped that Nat had not heard it mentioned at Bowford. But he needn't have worried, for the fellow merely grunted. "What are you doing in Cobham?"

Ned spoke up quickly. "She's my cousin, master. She's helping me get some things for—"

"I didn't ask you!" Nat growled, and jerked his thumb at Ben. "Let the maid speak for herself."

Ben struggled to think of an answer. Then an idea came to him: he would simply tell the truth. "We wanted to see the prisoner," he said in the best country accent he could manage.

Nat frowned. "What d'ye know about him?"

"Only rumours, master," Ben answered, struggling to give his voice a higher pitch. "How you brought 'im in all by yourself – a dangerous felon, too. 'Twas very brave of you!"

Nat gazed suspiciously at him. Ben heard Ned draw a breath at his boldness. But to his relief, Ben found that it had worked.

"You think I fear a man like that?" Nat sneered, sticking his chest out. "I could deal with three such, at one go!"

"Where is he?" Ben asked eagerly. "In the lean-to, back of Master Piggott's?"

Nat sniffed. "Nah...you're too late. The constable's took him to Guildford. He'll get what's coming to 'im, make no mistake about that!"

"You mean, he's going to be hanged?" Ned said, sensing Ben's dismay.

"He would if I had any say in it," Nat muttered. "Now, be on your way." He was about to move off, but Ben mastered himself and ventured another question.

"What did he steal?" he asked. Before Nat could reply he added: "I heard 'twas a sack of gold..."

At that Nat stiffened. "How d'you know he stole anything?" he demanded.

"Rumours." Ben shrugged.

"Well, you know where rumours lead, maid?" the squat fellow retorted. "They lead you into trouble, that's where. Now get along!" And before Ben could move, Nat gave him a shove in the chest that sent him staggering. With his thoughts in turmoil, he saw Ned already walking away, and hurried after him.

They returned to Bowford Manor, where Ben changed back into his own clothes. He wanted to be on his own, so he made his way to the kitchen garden. Ned seemed to understand, and left him alone. There was no one about, and Ben sat down outside the tool house, trying to collect his thoughts.

The news that Solomon had been taken to Guildford – the best part of ten miles away, according to Ned – was a shock. Now it seemed to Ben he still had two choices: he could stay at Bowford and keep searching for the Lodovico plate, or he could go and join the rest of the company at Oatlands. But finding the plate seemed such a hopeless task... Perhaps the best thing was to go to John, Hugh and the others after all; he missed them terribly. He tried to push away the awful feeling that had come over him, that he would never see Solomon again.

The afternoon was waning now, and Ben got up and started back towards the house. Then the thought struck him that even if he managed to ask permission of Sir James, he would probably not be allowed to leave until the next day. He passed the brick archway leading to the stable yard, thinking with a heavy heart of Lady Sarah's plan to find the Lodovico plate. Now Lady Sarah seemed far away, though he assumed she was still in the house, confined to her chamber. He remembered how they had met, four days ago, then he thought of her pony Tamora. He smiled slightly, thinking of how she had shouted at the groom and told him that Ben had permission to come and go as he pleased... He stopped. He did not expect to see Lady Sarah again, but at least he could go and say goodbye to Tamora.

He walked into the stable yard, and found nobody about. All the household seemed asleep on this warm afternoon, like the folk of Cobham. He stepped through the main doorway into the gloomy stable. But to his disappointment, Tamora was gone – in fact every stall was empty. All the horses must have been turned out into the paddock to graze... Suddenly, Ben heard hooves on the cobbles outside, along with men's voices. The next moment, without really knowing why, he had flung himself down in a corner and covered himself with hay.

Horseshoes echoed in the yard, then came footsteps as the men dismounted and led their horses into the stable. Through gaps in the hay, Ben could make out two figures... Then he gasped as he heard the voice of Sir Ralph.

"Where are the grooms – asleep? By heaven, if so they'll regret it!" he muttered, whereupon the other man spoke.

"You may leave your mount here. I'll go and seek them."

Ben froze: the voice was Thomas Bullen's.

"Not that surly fellow," Sir Ralph told him. "I'll

not have him touch my best horse!"

"As you wish," Bullen answered in a cold voice, which prompted an exasperated reply from the other.

"Oh, away with your injured pride, Bullen. Are you still smarting from this morning?"

There was a pause, then Bullen answered: "It's clear I've yet to earn your trust, Sir Ralph."

"Trust?" Sir Ralph snorted. "We've let you arrange everything! What further proof do you need?"

The horses stamped about, until Bullen settled them down. Sir Ralph was moving towards the doorway.

"You had that wretch of a player taken away pretty quick, did you not?" Bullen said. "Don't you think I know how to deal with him?"

Sir Ralph sighed. "It's not you I doubt, but Piggott," he said in a milder tone. "A fool like him could endanger the whole scheme, surely you can see that?"

"Of course I can," Bullen replied. "Which is why I wouldn't let him remove the plate, let alone that creature he keeps to do his dirty work."

He had moved closer to Sir Ralph. Ben could see their boots, only a few feet away. He kept as still as he could, and tried hard not to make a sound.

"Well, someone must move it, and soon," Sir Ralph said. He had lowered his voice, so that Ben could barely hear him. He strained to catch Bullen's answer.

"There's no cause for alarm," the steward muttered. "I'm certain Sir James knows nothing of the list—"

"Not yet, perhaps," Sir Ralph interrupted. "But who knows when he might hear rumours of it? I don't intend to wait any longer than necessary. There's too much at stake, for my sister and I!"

Both men moved out through the doorway, and whatever else they said was lost to Ben. He waited until he was sure they had left the yard, then scrambled out from his hiding place. As he tore the wisps of hay from his hair and face, he sneezed violently, startling the two horses. Then without further ado he hurried out. Luckily there was no one in the yard. He ducked through the archway and ran fast through the kitchen garden until he reached the tool house. There at last he stopped, sinking to the ground beside the door, his heart pounding – and not merely from running. For he knew that by sheer chance he had learned something of great importance, and only now did it strike him with full force: the Lodovico plate had not been taken away, after all – but was still here, somewhere at Bowford!

So now it had to be found – for Solomon's very life depended on it.

Master Henry had been right: Thomas Bullen was behind the theft – but the real instigator of it was Sir Ralph Gosson!

Chapter Twelve

That evening Ben took supper in the kitchen with the servants. Master Beech was away for the day and the other gardeners had gone off, locking the tool house. So Ben sat, his thoughts in turmoil, between Jane and another woman who talked over his head as if he weren't there. They had no idea how he felt, how he was bursting to tell someone what he had discovered. The plate was hidden, for all he knew somewhere close by – and Thomas Bullen, the man who had arrested Solomon for theft, had arranged everything. He had heard Sir Ralph use those very words.

The more he thought about the matter, the more anxious he grew. He must tell someone soon – tonight, in fact; but who could he trust? Keeping his eyes on his trencher, he chewed his food slowly while he considered. Lady Sarah was the obvious person, but she was still confined to her chamber. Ned had gone home to his family...which left only one other: Nan. She was Lady Sarah's friend, though Ben was not sure what she would be able to do. Then he drew a sudden breath, and a crumb of bread flew to the back of his throat, making him choke.

"Clumsy!" Jane gave him a hard look. "Come on, cough it up."

Ben got up from the bench, still coughing. The other servants glanced at him, then carried on with their chatter. Gradually he got his breath back. "I'm all right," he gasped. "I...I'll go out and get some air."

Jane shrugged, and turned away.

The reason for the choking was that Ben had realized who was the best person to tell: the one who knew as much about the plate as anyone – and perhaps about the "list", too, whatever that was: Henry Godfrey. Henry had wanted to tell Sir James everything; now he must do so, without delay. Whatever trouble Ben might get into, he must go and find him at once.

He glanced at the path which led out of the kitchen gardens and past the side door of the house. If it were open he could slip inside, and climb the stairs to the tutor's chamber... He hesitated, then noticed that someone was standing only a few yards away. He whirled about, to see a familiar figure by the door of the wash house.

"Nan!" He gave a sigh of relief, then saw the frown on her face.

"What are you doing?" Nan asked sharply.

"I've got to find Master Henry," Ben told her. "At once..."

He turned to go – but quickly Nan took a step towards him. "Don't be a fool," she said. "If you're caught in the house, heaven knows what'll happen to you."

"I don't care," Ben said impatiently. But Nan quickly grabbed him by the arm, and before he knew what was happening, she had pushed him into the wash house.

"Let me go!" he cried. "I have to tell Henry about the plate!"

"What about the plate?"

"It's still here," Ben answered. "At Bowford!"

Nan's eyes narrowed, but she said nothing. So Ben went on: "I overheard something... I must tell Henry.

Do you know where he is?"

Nan shrugged. "At his books, I'd say..." She seemed to collect herself, and fixed Ben with a piercing look. "What is it you overheard?"

"Sir Ralph and Master Bullen talking," Ben told her. "He arranged everything – Bullen, that is. They didn't trust The Pig or Nat to take it, so..." He broke off, realizing he was not making much sense. He took a breath and tried to calm down.

"I didn't understand all of it," he went on. "But Master Henry will unravel it – I'm sure he will."

Nan was standing very still. "Well, Ben Button," she said at last, "it seems you're quite a...what-do-they-call-it? Quite an intelligencer."

Ben blinked. "That's a spy, isn't it?"

Nan gave a wry smile. "I suppose it is – someone who ferrets things out. I should call you *the ferret*."

"If you like," Ben replied. "But I have to tell Master Henry. I must go to the house..."

"No, you mustn't. Aren't you in enough trouble already?" Nan thought for a moment. "I'll go," she said. "I can find a reason to be on the upper floors... and I know where the tutor's room is."

Ben's spirits rose. "Then please don't delay," he urged. "I'm sure they're going to move the plate soon." He frowned. "If only I knew where it might be..."

"Quiet!" Nan stepped to the doorway, poked her head out and turned to him. "You'd best keep your head down, before someone notices what you're up to. Let Henry deal with it. I'll go and look for him. Now get yourself back to the kitchen!"

Ben hurried out. He returned to the kitchen to find the servants had gone from the table, along with the food. Nobody paid him much attention, and soon afterwards he went to the tool house and found it unlocked. Feeling very tired, Ben went to his bed. But the events of the day had made him restless, and in the dead of night he awoke, hearing owls calling from the wood – and once, what sounded like the cry of some wild animal. He turned over and went back to sleep.

The morning was cloudy, and no sooner had Ben eaten breakfast than Tom Beech sent for him. His face was grave.

"I've something to say to 'ee, boy," he announced. "I'm ordered to, by Lady Anne herself. It's…your punishment."

With all the excitement of yesterday, Ben had almost forgotten his unpleasant encounter with Lady Anne by the stairs. His heart gave a jolt.

Beech cleared his throat. "She says, if you was thinking of changing your mind and going to join your fellows at Oatlands, the offer's withdrawn. You're to stay here till further notice."

The old gardener turned and spat into a soil bed. When he turned back, Ben saw how uncomfortable he looked. "Like I say," he muttered, "I was ordered to tell ye."

Ben lowered his eyes. Was he under suspicion now? He was sure nobody had seen him at the stables yesterday. And as for his visit to Cobham in disguise, he was certain that only Ned knew about it. Surely if anyone could be trusted, Ned could?

Tom Beech was regarding him with a kindly expression. "Chin up, boy – it could be worse," he said. "I'll wager a week's pay your fellows will be back for ye before long. A good prentice is worth 'is weight in gold, isn't that so?"

Ben felt very disheartened. He made no reply.

"Meanwhile," Beech went on, "you've got bed and board, and work to keep ye busy – in the fresh air, too! There's many would be glad of that."

Ben tried to smile, whereupon the gardener spoke up. "Would ye like to come and look at the bees?"

"I didn't know there were any," Ben said.

"Oh, aye." Beech nodded. "I'm head gardener,

fruit picker, bee-keeper and who knows what else. Bowford's jack of all trades, that's Tom Beech." With a jerk of his head, he stamped off along the path.

The two of them crossed to the far side of the garden. There was a fence with a little gate Ben had not noticed before. They went through into an orchard, from where he could already hear a loud humming. It struck him that here was another part of the manor he didn't know existed. How vast the place was... He tried once again to push away the thought that the plate could never be found. Perhaps it made no difference whether Nan had told Master Henry about it, after all...

His shoes swishing through long grass, he followed Tom Beech to a group of beehives, placed a few feet apart in a clearing among apple trees. They were made of woven straw, like upturned baskets, and stood on little wooden tables.

"I fashion the skeps myself," Beech said proudly. "Sir James is fond of his honeybees, like Lady Catherine was. Now, you'd best stay back in case they get angry."

Ben watched while he went to the nearest hive, lifted its edge carefully and looked underneath. Bees flew about his head, but he did not seem troubled by them. He straightened up, then moved to the other hives and looked under each in turn. "Bees seem content," he said. "I won't blow smoke in today... The smoke makes 'em think there's a fire, so they fill themselves with honey quick, to build their strength. Then when you handle them, they don't sting."

"My uncle has bees, back home in my village," Ben said. "I've watched him take the honeycombs out."

Beech looked surprised. "You mean you're a country boy? I thought all you player folk hailed from London."

"I live there," Ben told him. "Just outside the city walls, in Bishopsgate. But I'm from Hornsey – that's in Middlesex."

"Then there's more to you than meets the eye, I can see that," Beech said. He gestured to the gate. "Let's get back. There's watering to do..." He squinted up at the sky. "We could do with a drop of rain."

They walked out of the orchard and along the border of the kitchen garden, towards the small pond where the gardeners filled their watering cans. But as they approached Ben saw two figures waving their arms.

Tom Beech frowned. "What's bothering them?" he muttered. He quickened his pace, and Ben did the same. Soon they reached the edge of the pond where the other gardeners stood. The look on the men's faces told them something was wrong. And the next moment, they saw what it was.

In the pond, a body was floating.

Ben stared, feeling a chill run up his spine. He had seen dead bodies before; few people had not, especially during times of plague. But to see one here in the kitchen garden, on a summer's day, was a terrible shock. His mouth went dry.

Tom Beech was also staring, grim-faced. At last, gesturing to the other men, he stepped into the shallow water. The three of them waded thigh-deep into the pond, and took hold of the man's legs – for by his clothing it was clearly a man, though he was face down. Slowly they drew the body to the edge, then lifted it carefully onto the path and turned it over.

But Ben had already seen the holes in the elbows of the black doublet; and even before the face appeared, pale and lifeless with the eyes wide open, he knew who it was.

Lady Sarah's tutor, Henry Godfrey.

Chapter Thirteen

The rest of that cloudy Monday passed quickly. Almost at once, the news spread through Bowford Manor that Lady Sarah's tutor had fallen into the pond and drowned. But Ben, who was sent off to weed the vegetable beds, did not believe it for one moment. He remembered the conversation in the schoolroom, when Henry had told Ben and Lady Sarah what danger he might be in. He had not turned up in a ditch with his throat cut, but in a shallow pond in the kitchen garden, a place he never went to. How many people, Ben wondered, truly believed that it was an accident?

All morning he went about his work, but his sharp eyes saw what went on. Thomas Bullen came down to the pond, and gave orders for the body to be taken away. He and Tom Beech talked for a while, and the two men who had made the discovery were called over for questioning. But it looked as if they could add little to what was already known, and finally Ben saw the steward walk off back to the house.

At midday when everyone went to take their meal Ben lingered behind, saying he was not hungry. He had been doing some hard thinking. Though it shocked him to believe it, he suspected that Sir Ralph and Bullen – the "plotters" as he now called them – were behind Master Henry's death. Somehow they had learned that he knew about the Lodovico plate. And now, Ben was afraid: not only was he up against murderers, he began to think that he too might be in danger. True, he had only told Nan what he had overheard in the stable, and she had said she would find Henry and tell him... His heart skipped a beat. Surely she would not have told anyone else? Was she really his friend, after all?

It was all becoming more dangerous than Ben had ever imagined. He needed to get to John, Hugh and the others and tell them everything. They, at least, he knew he could trust. But now he had been told he couldn't leave – he had to remain here, like a prisoner!

Leaving his tools, he walked to the end of the garden, near to the brewhouse. He tried to summon all his courage, as he had done that first time he set foot upon a stage, back in London. And he formed a resolve, that he would not stay a day longer. He would escape from Bowford, make his way to Oatlands and find his company. He realized he could tell no one about his plan, not even Ned Stiles. He must go alone, tonight. Perhaps if he tore his clothes and dirtied them, he could disguise himself as a beggar child...

"Ben!"

A low, but familiar voice called out. Ben looked round and saw no one. Then he guessed where it came from, and went quickly to the brewhouse. As he stepped into the gloomy interior, a slight figure in a blue gown stood up from the corner where she had been crouching.

"Lady Sarah!" Ben stared. "What are you doing here?"

He was alarmed to see how pale and taut her face was. Without answering she went to the doorway and peered out, then turned. "You know what's happened to poor Henry?"

Ben saw that her eyes were filled with tears. Awkwardly he put out a hand as if to comfort her, but she flinched away.

"Someone's murdered him, Ben," she said in a small voice. "And now, Lady Anne won't let me see my father at all!"

The two of them sat on empty barrels and talked. Quickly, Ben told Lady Sarah all that had happened, but even the removal of Solomon to Guildford seemed unimportant, compared to her news.

"What did you mean," he asked, "when you said Lady Anne won't let you see your father?"

"She says he's ill," Lady Sarah told him. "He keeps to his chamber, and when I ask to see him Lady Anne turns me away. She says he needs careful nursing, and she must do it herself..." She trailed off. "Now, you tell me Uncle Ralph is part of the scheme to steal the plate." She shook her head. "I've never liked him, but I never thought he was such a villain as that. And with Henry dead, I don't know who to trust!"

"How did you get out without being seen?" Ben asked. He was thinking fast.

"I stole the spare key to my closet," Lady Sarah

replied. "I can get through there to the empty chamber next to mine, and onto the landing above the side stairs."

"Could you get away tonight?" Ben asked. "I mean, after dark?"

She drew breath sharply. "Do you have a plan?"

Now, Ben had made his mind up. "Yes. We'll go together," he answered firmly. "That is, if you still trust me...?"

After a moment she managed a little smile, looking more like the Lady Sarah he had first met when she challenged him that afternoon with her bow and arrow.

"I do," she said.

That night, Ben couldn't have slept even if he had wanted to. He lay in the darkness of the tool house, waiting until he heard snoring from the prentice gardeners. When he judged the time to be right, he got up softly from his pallet. Carefully he placed a sack stuffed with weeds under his blanket and ruffled it to look like a sleeping form. Then he slung his pack over his shoulder, and stole towards the door. Thankfully the gardeners kept the hinges well oiled, so that he was able to open it silently. The next moment he was out in the chilly night air, and it was pitch-dark.

He walked through the kitchen garden, trying to adjust his eyes to the gloom. Lights showed from the upper floors of the manor. The path was visible, a pale sliver of gravel. He made his way to the side of the house and waited, hoping that Lady Sarah would be able to slip away as arranged. He did not know the time, but guessed it to be almost midnight. After a while the clouds parted and the moon poked through, illuminating the bulk of the great house above him. Then suddenly he shivered – and not merely from the chill.

Someone had come out of an outhouse door and was standing in the yard, very still, as if listening. Ben peered, crouching by the garden wall... The figure turned, and he saw the face. It was Nan the washerwoman.

Then it was all he could do not to cry out, for he heard footsteps, coming rapidly around the house by the side path. In seconds they would pass within a few feet of Ben. All he could think of was to make himself as small as possible, and flatten himself against the wall.

A man strode past, his dark cloak flowing behind him, and walked straight up to Nan. The fellow glanced round to make sure he was not being observed, then spoke to her. Ben's heart thudded: though he couldn't hear the words, he saw the gleam of a bald head in the moonlight – and recognized the steward, Thomas Bullen.

He watched, scarcely believing his eyes, as Nan disappeared inside the wash house. And then an idea struck Ben, that made his blood run cold. He thought back four days, to when he and Lady Sarah had begun their search for the Lodovico plate. They had tracked it from the great hall to the kitchens, and out the back door…and now, he saw that the most obvious place to hide the plate had been right under their noses: the wash house! A dreadful feeling of betrayal came over him, as he realized for certain that Nan, too, must be part of the plot to steal the plate!

Bullen waited impatiently, until Nan reappeared with something wrapped in a cloth. But even as Ben saw Bullen take the object from her and turn away, there came another sound from his right, and he swung round in alarm. Lady Sarah had arrived – at the worst possible time!

Bullen was walking swiftly towards Ben, just as the figure of Lady Sarah appeared at the side door, carrying what looked like a bundle of clothing. Now the steward would see her, and their escape would be foiled.

There was no time to think of the consequences. As Bullen drew abreast of him, still crouching by the wall, Ben jumped up and stuck his foot out. With a cry the steward tripped and fell headlong, landing heavily on the path. The wrapped object flew from his grasp, and in a second Ben had caught it up and was running to the side door, where Lady Sarah stood with her hand to her mouth.

"Run!" he cried.

He grabbed her by the hand and pulled her along the path. But he had forgotten her long gown: Lady Sarah's foot caught in the edge, causing her to stumble and fall to her knees. Without a sound she got up, picked up her skirts and started to run. In her other hand she still clutched her bundle.

The two of them skirted the wall of the stable yard and reached the paddock. The fence was visible in the moonlight, and beyond it the horses milled about, snickering nervously. As they climbed the fence, Lady Sarah turned to Ben.

"If we can saddle Tamora—"

"There isn't time!" he shouted back. "We must get to the Cobham road, then find somewhere to hide!"

They jumped down from the fence and ran across

the paddock, scattering the horses. Ben had not dared to look back – but now from the direction of the house he heard a shout, followed by another. He gritted his teeth. They would be pursued, of course, and their chances were slim. Clutching his precious cargo, the hard edge of which he could feel through the cloth, he ran to the far gate. To his relief Lady Sarah was not only keeping up – she was overtaking him.

They reached the gate and slammed it behind them. Then they were climbing the hill that overlooked the Mole valley, running side by side through the long grass. In a matter of minutes, both panting for breath, they had reached the summit and were running down the other side. The great house disappeared behind them. They gained the road, faintly visible in the moonlight, then ran along it until they were so breathless they had to slow to a walk. Only now did they look at one another, scared but relieved...and at once, both of them burst into nervous laughter. It had not quite gone to plan: but somehow, they had made their escape from Bowford Manor.

Chapter Fourteen

*I*t did not take them long to reach Cobham. Not even a dog barked as the two young people walked softly through the village. Ben led the way, past the White Lion Inn and down to the riverside, where The Pig's cottage looked as dark and silent as the others. Luckily the moon was out, and the footbridge over the river was clearly visible.

Lady Sarah was tired now, and limping slightly, though she made no complaint. Ben urged her on until they had crossed the wooden bridge and gained the far bank. Some distance away a great hill rose, black against the night sky.

Here they stopped, and Lady Sarah turned to him. "That's St. George's Hill," she said. "I wouldn't like to walk by there in the dark..." She shivered. "It could be dangerous."

Then she looked at the object Ben had been carrying under his arm, and her eyes lit up. "Is that what I think it is?"

"Let's wait until we get off the road," Ben said, still afraid they had been followed. "Then we'll see, shall we?"

Lady Sarah was staring. "We should unwrap it and make sure it's the plate," she said. And she reached out to take it from Ben.

"It has to be," Ben told her. "We must keep moving..." He trailed off, for Lady Sarah was wearing a stubborn look. She held her hands out, until reluctantly Ben gave her the precious object. She fumbled with the cords that bound it, until she had opened an edge of the cloth. She peered inside, then looked up at Ben excitedly.

"It is! It's the Lodovico plate!" Her eyes shone in the moonlight. "How on earth did you find it?"

"You might say it fell into my hands," Ben answered. "Now please, My Lady – can we keep going, and look at it properly tomorrow? We're not safe yet!"

Lady Sarah didn't argue further, but handed the plate back. Ben looked around quickly. The road snaked away into darkness, and he wasn't sure if it was the right one.

"Do you know which direction Oatlands is?" he asked.

Lady Sarah considered. "North, I think," she answered. "It's beside the Thames, like all the Queen's palaces, so she can travel by river." She looked up at the sky. "This road goes north."

"How do you know?"

"The moon's behind us, to the south, and the North Star's ahead."

"Then let's go a little way along the road, at least," Ben said. "There might be somewhere we can shelter."

She looked anxious. "You think they'll follow us here?"

"I think they'll scour the whole county for us, My Lady," Ben answered. Suddenly he too felt tired. He longed to sit down on the grass verge and rest, but he knew they could not. He faced her again. "Can you walk a bit further?"

Lady Sarah sighed, and gave a nod.

*

After a further half-hour's walking, they were both exhausted. Cobham was far behind, and there seemed to be nothing but open country ahead. Then as Lady Sarah was on the point of sinking down by the roadside, Ben saw a dark shape some distance away. Without a word he took her arm and dragged her towards it. It proved to be an old thatched barn, almost derelict. The door was open, and there was nothing inside but weeds growing up from the floor. With the last of their strength the two fugitives heaved the door shut, threw down their packs and sank to the ground, to fall into a deep sleep that lasted until dawn.

Ben awoke with a start, thinking he heard voices. For a moment, he could not think where he was, then memories of the flight from Bowford Manor flooded back. He sat up and glanced round. Nearby Lady Sarah slept soundly, huddled in her blue gown which was now torn and soiled. Her hair had come loose, and stuck out in all directions. Truly, Ben thought, the pair of them looked almost like beggar children already.

Suddenly he thought of the Lodovico plate, and looked wildly about. Then seeing that it was right beside him, he let out a sigh of relief.

There was no sound but birdsong. The sun's first

rays were beginning to poke through the thatch above Ben's head. The barn's roof was full of holes, and they were lucky it hadn't rained. Ben got to his knees, leaned over and shook Lady Sarah gently.

"Wake up, My Lady," he said.

Lady Sarah stirred, and half opened her eyes. "Kat?" she murmured. "Is that you?"

"No," Ben answered, "it's me."

She gasped and sat up, eyes wide. Then her memory came back. "Oh..." Her face fell. "I thought it was Kat, my maid, come to wash and dress me."

"I'm afraid there's nowhere to wash," Ben said, managing a smile. "As for dressing, we'll have to do something about our clothes soon. Then we must be on our way."

Lady Sarah sighed. "Did you manage to bring anything to eat?" she asked, rather grumpily.

"No, I didn't think of it," Ben admitted.

"Fortunately for us both, I did," Lady Sarah told him. Opening her bundle, she pulled out something wrapped in a napkin and unfolded it to reveal a small, round loaf.

"Well," Ben said. "Today, that looks like a feast."

While they shared the bread, they talked about last night and all that had happened. At first, when Ben told Lady Sarah that it appeared Nan the washerwoman had been part of the scheme to steal the plate, she refused to believe him.

"Nan's my friend – has been ever since I was a little girl," she cried. "She would never betray me!"

But she fell silent, once Ben had told her what he had seen. She seemed to be struggling with herself. Finally she glanced round, and saw how unhappy Ben looked.

"What right have you to look so gloomy?" she demanded. "I'm the one who's been betrayed... I've lost the two people I cared most about – apart from my father – Henry, and now Nan!"

But Ben was feeling thoroughly miserable. For now it seemed to him that it was because of his actions that Henry had been murdered. He hesitated, then drew a deep breath and told Lady Sarah of his fears: that Henry had been killed because he knew too much, about the plate and about Bullen – perhaps he had even guessed of Sir Ralph's involvement too.

To his relief Lady Sarah listened, and gradually her expression softened to one of sympathy.

"It wasn't your fault," she said finally. "Henry knew the danger – you remember what he said to us in the schoolroom."

"But I never thought it would really happen," Ben said. "When I saw him floating in the pond like that..."

"Don't speak of it!" Lady Sarah was on her feet suddenly. "If you recall, Henry wanted to go to my father and tell him everything – it was I who stopped him!"

She looked away. And now it was Ben's turn to try and comfort her. "This is silly, both of us blaming ourselves," he said. Then he sighed. "If only one of us had guessed that the plate was under our noses the whole time – in the wash house!"

But now he saw that Lady Sarah was no longer listening. Instead she was gazing at the tightly wrapped object lying nearby. "And now, we have it," she said softly. "I can hardly believe the way it fell into our hands like that. It's high time we looked at it properly – and this time I'm not taking 'no' for an answer!"

Ben hesitated. "Should we not disguise ourselves first, My Lady, in case someone comes along?" he asked. But Lady Sarah was wearing her stubborn face.

So together they took the heavy object and began to undo the cords with which it was bound. Soon they were unfolding the linen covering, both growing more and more excited. And when the beautiful dish finally appeared, it was all Ben could do not to gasp aloud.

The Lodovico plate.

He gazed at it, thinking it would be better described as a shallow golden bowl. It was finely ornamented with leaf-shaped panels of blue and white enamel, and engraved with intricate designs. For the moment, both Ben and Lady Sarah forgot their surroundings. They pored over the precious plate, which had been the cause of so much trouble, including the arrest of one man, and now, the death of another. What famous hands had it passed through; what stories could it tell? With wonder, Ben's fingers traced the interwoven patterns of flowers and branches that ran round its edge.

And though she knew the treasured object well enough, Lady Sarah seemed no less intrigued than he was. She pointed out features of its design to Ben. "These are fleurs-de-lis," she told him. "And these are olive leaves…and these jewels set in the rim are agates." Taking the plate in both hands, she turned it over. The tracery work continued over the edge, onto the underside of the plate, where it petered out near the base.

"So somewhere in this design is a hidden message of some sort?" Ben peered at it, frowning. "I can't see any sign of it – let alone a list."

Lady Sarah frowned too. "I knew nothing of any list until you told me of it," she admitted. She let go of the plate, and sat back heavily. "It's all like some dreadful nightmare," she said. "My uncle plotting with Bullen, to steal it...and now Henry's murder!" She turned to Ben with an anxious look. "I'd no idea how important the plate was. But if they've resorted to such desperate measures to get their hands on it, then it must be. And the more I think about it, the more I'm sure Lady Anne's a part of the scheme. I just know she is – and now I've left my father in her clutches!"

Ben took a deep breath, and put the plate back in its covering. "Our best chance is to get to Oatlands as soon as we can," he said. "My company will help us, and so will Lord Bonner. He's famous at court, and respected by the Queen herself. My master John trusts him completely – and that's good enough for me."

Lady Sarah seemed to recover her courage. "I hope you're right." She got to her feet. "You spoke of disguises," she said. "So I brought a few things with me."

She fumbled in her bundle, and drew out a clean linen shift and hood. "They're my maid's," she said. "Do you think I will pass for a beggar in them?"

Ben tried to keep a straight face. "I...I think they will serve, My Lady," he answered. "Only, I fear we may have to roughen them up a little."

Lady Sarah made no reply, whereupon he added:

"Perhaps you'd like to wait until I've fashioned my own disguise, then see for yourself?"

She watched as Ben fumbled in his own pack, before realizing how embarrassed he was. Finally she sighed. "Would you like me to turn my back while you change?" And she turned round and sat down.

Relieved, Ben went to work. And if Lady Sarah's curiosity was aroused by sounds of tearing, scraping and scuffling, she kept her back to him until he said he was ready. Then she stood up and faced about, and her mouth fell open.

If it was Ben Button, she did not recognize him. Instead of the fresh-faced boy player she knew, there stood a shambling figure in rags, with matted hair and a face almost black with dirt. She drew a deep breath.

"And you wish me to look like that, too?"

"Yes – otherwise you will be recognized," Ben answered. "Please try to think of the danger we're in. Already there will be riders out from Bowford. It's only a matter of time before they follow us here."

For a long time Lady Sarah said nothing. Then taking the snow-white shift in both hands, she tore it as hard as she could. She went on making tears, then stopped. But when Ben reached out to take it from her, she shook her head.

"I can dirty it myself," she told him.

Ben watched as she bent down and rubbed the shift on the ground, making a dark patch. Then she stood up, saw him trying to hide a smile, and flushed.

"What's wrong?" she demanded.

"I think you should let me do it, My Lady," he said.

"Do you indeed!" Lady Sarah glared at him. "You think you're mighty clever, don't you, Ben Button? You think it takes brains to dirty an old smock?"

Ben blinked. "I'm more used to changing my appearance than you are, that's all," he answered.

Lady Sarah tossed her head. But finally she lowered her gaze, and held out the shift. Ben took it from her, dropped it and began grinding it into the earth floor with his heel.

Chapter Fifteen

An hour later, as the sun climbed above the poplar trees beside the road, two small, ragged figures could be seen walking along it, heading north. A passer-by might have been moved to put a penny in the dirty cap the boy held, even if the girl by his side looked a little too well-fed for a beggar child. They might have wondered why the two children were alone, and not part of a larger group which was how such folk usually travelled. But then, like most passers-by, they would probably have shrugged and gone on their way.

For Ben, the journey could not pass quickly enough. Every few minutes he looked back, expecting to see horsemen thundering towards them. In his heart he knew their disguises would not fool anyone for long – especially one who knew Lady Sarah. At any moment his plan could fail, and he would likely find himself being accused of kidnapping and dragged back to Bowford – or worse, to Cobham, to be at the mercy of The Pig and his terrible henchman.

But gradually, he began to admire Lady Sarah. She bore her filthy disguise without a murmur, and kept walking even though her ankle still pained her from the fall at Bowford. Along with her torn shift, Ben had dirtied her face with earth from the barn floor, and rubbed her hair and hands with it for good measure – and she had not uttered a word of protest. Her fine blue gown they had left behind, along with Ben's pack which looked too good for a beggar's. The most precious thing – indeed, the only precious thing they carried – was strapped tightly to Ben's body under his shirt, with strips torn from Lady Sarah's shift. It was heavy, and it made him very uneasy. He knew that there many sorts of villains on the roads: priggers who went on foot, and prancers who rode, any of whom would not scruple to steal his last penny. What they might do if they discovered the Lodovico plate, he did not want to imagine.

And soon, they had their first moment of danger. Almost before they heard him, a horseman came cantering up the dusty road behind them. Lady Sarah caught Ben's eye, knowing that she was to remain silent, otherwise her educated voice would give her away. She kept her eyes on the ground as the man drew alongside them, and slowed his big Barbary horse to a halt.

At once Ben turned to him, holding out his cap. "Penny for a poor orphan, sir?" he whined.

The man was tall, and looked like a soldier. He wore a leather jerkin, and over it a steel breastplate, the sort called a cuirass. Ben tried to ignore the sword that swung from his saddle, and concentrated on trying to act his part.

"What are you doing here?" the fellow demanded.

Ben kept his cap held out before him. "Just travelling, master," he answered. "My sister and I…"

"Travelling to where?" The man was frowning. "Do you not know where this road leads?"

Ben shook his head. "We're strangers to these parts."

The big man looked him up and down, then turned his gaze upon Lady Sarah, whose eyes remained downcast. There was a tense moment, before to their relief the fellow sighed and fumbled for the purse at his belt.

"I'd advise you to go left when the road forks," he said. "Otherwise you'll find yourselves at the gates of Oatlands. The Queen herself is in residence – and her guards deal harshly with vagabonds."

He threw down a coin, then shook the reins. The big horse leaped forward, and the man disappeared in a cloud of dust.

"The cheek of the fellow!"

Ben turned sharply, to see that Lady Sarah was fuming. She stared at the road ahead and stamped her foot. "If only my father were here!" she cried. "He'd make that ruffian eat his words! Calling me a vagabond..." She broke off suddenly, and looked shamefaced at Ben.

"I ask your pardon," she said. "I...I believe I forgot myself."

Ben smiled. "You did well, My Lady," he said. "See – we've got a penny for our pains!"

He picked up the coin. Lady Sarah stared at it, then at him. "I've never tried to be anyone besides myself before," she said. "But this is how you live your life, isn't it?" When Ben merely shrugged, she asked: "Were you afraid?"

Ben nodded. "Were you?"

She thought for a moment. "Yes," she replied. "And now I wonder what will happen when we get to Oatlands, and I tell them who I am. Suppose they don't believe me?"

Ben hesitated, then thumped himself on the chest. There was a dull sound, as his fist thudded against the Lodovico plate.

"We have this," he said. "I only hope they don't think we've stolen it…"

Soon, they came to the fork in the road, as the horseman had told them they would; and very quickly, matters took a different turn.

Back from the road to their left stood a clump of trees, with what looked like a group of people sitting beneath them. There was no mistaking where the right fork led: in the distance they could see gates, and beyond them an impressive-looking building with towers: the royal palace of Oatlands.

Now both of them felt nervous. Ben had tried to push away the thought that Lady Sarah might be right: that when the two of them presented themselves at the palace gates they would be turned away – or even arrested for begging without a licence.

He had not thought of it when he first formed his escape plan, back in the brewhouse at Bowford.

"Perhaps if we tried to clean ourselves up a little, My Lady," he began, then stopped. Lady Sarah was staring past him, at the road behind them.

"It's too late," she said.

He whirled about, hearing the sound of hooves, and saw what he had dreaded: horsemen, approaching rapidly. Though they were some distance away he fancied their leader wore brown and rode a fine hunting horse...

There was nothing else for it: he grabbed Lady Sarah's hand and hurried her off the road, towards the trees. But his notion of hiding until the riders had passed gave way to dismay. For now he saw that the group sitting in the shade staring at them were as raggedly dressed as he and Lady Sarah; in fact, their appearance was far worse. For their rags were genuine: the clothes worn almost to shreds, patched and re-patched and stained with months of travel. Their bare limbs carried sores, and the faces...

Their faces were not dirty like Ben's and Lady Sarah's. They were tanned and weather-beaten, ravaged with disease and pinched with hunger. One man had a filthy bandage round his head, another wore an eye patch. Lady Sarah shrank back, but Ben gripped her hand tightly and bent his mouth to her ear.

"We must try to hide among the beggars," he breathed. "It's our only chance!"

And to his relief Lady Sarah relented, and allowed him to lead her towards the palliards: true beggars born to the life, who had no other home than the open road and the sky. As the two drew close, they saw there were about a dozen in the group; men, women and children, some little more than babies, others of middle years; and one, the oldest by far, grey-headed and wizened. And it was this man who got stiffly to his feet, waving at them. He seemed to be shooing them away. His other hand gripped the wooden crutch on which he now leaned. His leg, they saw, was misshapen and hung uselessly.

They stopped, hearing the horses close behind, both praying silently that they would pass. But it was not to be: the hoof-beats slowed, sending a cloud of dust blowing over Ben's and Lady Sarah's heads towards the beggar folk. Ben braced himself, waiting for the shout that would come at any moment, ordering him to turn around. And then it would all be over. His spirits sank: their flight was doomed – had been from the start. And what help could he expect from a rabble of beggars?

Then he froze. For the grey-headed man was not waving them away: he was waving them forward, urgently. The two of them hurried towards him, as the old man took a clumsy step of his own. And at last, he spoke.

"Sit down quick, you little fools!" he hissed. "And let me do the talking!"

Chapter Sixteen

They sat huddled together in the middle of the group, and quickly a woman moved towards them. Ben stiffened, but the woman merely threw a dirty, torn cloak about their shoulders. "Draw it close," she muttered, "and don't look up."

Each of them took an edge of the cloak and held onto it. The eyes of every person in the group except Ben and Lady Sarah were now upon the riders, who were walking their horses towards them. They stopped, and their leader stared down at the old man. He wore a look of haughty distaste which Ben would have recognized easily, if he had dared to look.

"Are you the leader of this band of rogues?" Sir Ralph Gosson snapped.

Beneath the cloak, Ben felt Lady Sarah flinch. He found her hand, and squeezed it tightly.

The old man bowed. "I am, Your Lordship," he answered, in an accent Ben did not know. "Llewellyn is my name."

"We seek two fugitives – a boy and a girl," Sir Ralph told him. "And there were two children by the road just now..."

"Ours, My Lord," the old man said quickly. "I've told them a hundred times not to stray. They will be punished for it!"

He jerked his head towards Ben and Lady Sarah. The silence that followed was the longest Ben had known in his life. For what seemed an age he kept his eyes on the ground, one hand gripping the cloak and the other holding Lady Sarah's hand tightly. He hardly dared to breathe.

Then suddenly, like a cloud the danger passed. Sir Ralph had been frowning at the tousled heads that poked out of the cloak, before deciding that two such dirty wretches could not possibly be Lady Sarah and Ben Button. With an oath, he swung his horse and barked an order to the men behind him.

"We've delayed enough," he cried. "We'll ride on to Weybridge – and I'll search every house if I have to!"

Then he dug his heels into the big horse's flanks and urged it away. The other Bowford men followed, raising more dust as they thundered down the road, taking the left-hand fork. In a short time, they were gone.

At last, Ben and Lady Sarah dared to look at each other. Then they let the cloak fall, and stood up. Lady Sarah gazed at the old man, but seemed lost for words. So it was Ben who spoke for them both.

"We're truly grateful to you," he said.

Now that the horsemen had gone, the group began to stir. Babies whined, while the older children gathered round the two newcomers, staring at them.

The man called Llewellyn looked down at Ben. "Whatever you've done," he said, "we wouldn't hand you over to such as those." He seemed to smile, though with his eyes rather than with his mouth. "What is it you've done, anyway?"

Ben hesitated, but Lady Sarah found her voice at last.

"We've taken nothing that was not rightfully ours," she answered. "We are on our way to Oatlands, to seek justice."

"Justice?" The old man peered at her. "What kind

of justice is it you hope to find there?" A ripple of laughter spread through some of the group.

"We cannot say," Ben replied. "I only hope that our luck holds."

He broke off, because Lady Sarah had put a hand on his arm. "One day, sir," she said to Llewellyn, "I will have someone seek you out, so that you may be rewarded for your kindness to me today. I will not forget it."

The old man's eyes widened. "It's a long time since anyone spoke such fair words to me," he murmured. "But think what you do. You'll get naught at Oatlands – unless it be a whipping."

Lady Sarah made no answer. Then with a glance at Ben, she said goodbye to the old man and the other beggars, before walking off towards the road. Ben nodded his farewell, and followed her. When he looked back a few minutes later, he saw only a huddle of dark shapes under the trees. To the passer-by they might have been deer or cattle, or perhaps merely shadows. Of Llewellyn, there was no sign.

Now Oatlands loomed ahead of them. As the Queen's palaces went this was in fact one of the smallest – smaller even than Bowford Manor. But still the gates were big and heavy, with a high wall stretching away on both sides. And before the gates stood two burly guards in helmets, armed with halberds.

Ben and Lady Sarah gazed at the walls, and at the palace beyond. High above their heads the red and gold royal standard was flying. "So the Queen really is in residence," Lady Sarah said. "I wasn't sure if that fellow spoke the truth." The two of them were standing under a tree beside the road, and the guards had not seen them. But Ben was looking worried.

"Supposing we wait until nightfall?" Lady Sarah suggested.

He frowned. "And then do what?"

"I could distract them, while you climb over the wall."

Ben's mouth fell open. "Are you mad?"

"I beg your pardon?" Lady Sarah's stubborn look was back. "Do you forget who I am?"

Ben was tired, and this time his temper snapped. "How could I, when you keep reminding me of it?" he asked hotly.

Lady Sarah drew a sharp breath, but before she could reply, he mastered himself quickly and held up his hands.

"Your pardon, *My Lady*," he muttered.

After a moment Lady Sarah gave a nod. And Ben's

heart sank, for he saw that she was already warming to her foolish idea.

"It's the obvious plan though, isn't it?" she enquired. "I go up to the guards saying I bear an important message, or something. Meanwhile you hide in the shadow of that oak tree there. You can shin up it and reach the wall; the branches are long enough."

Ben was almost lost for words. "Do you realize what you're saying, My Lady?" he asked, trying to keep a respectful tone. "There'll be guards everywhere, and dogs, and—"

"I asked you once before if you were a coward, Ben Button," Lady Sarah interrupted. "Do I need to ask you again?"

He swallowed, feeling a cold hand clutching at his heart.

"No, My Lady," he replied. Then he moved to the other side of the tree, and sat down heavily with his back to it.

Night came slowly, but not slowly enough for Ben Button. All day he and Lady Sarah had watched the comings and goings at Oatlands from a safe distance. Now at last they must put the plan into effect, and Ben did not like it one little bit. He comforted himself with the hope that Lord Bonner's men were still somewhere in the palace, and they at least would vouch for him – provided of course, that he could get inside.

In the darkness he had crept to the foot of the big tree near the wall. Here he crouched, until Lady Sarah appeared, marching boldly towards the gates. He had to admire her nerve: she did not flinch, even when the guards quickly lowered their halberds, shouting at her to halt.

She had washed her face in a stream, and tidied her appearance as best she could, but she still looked like a vagabond. Ben could not hear the conversation that followed; nor did he wish to. He peered upwards, and began to climb the tree, grateful for its thick foliage. Soon he was level with the top of the wall, and working his way along a stout branch towards it. Lights blazed from the palace windows, but he was not here to admire such sights. Quickly he eased himself forwards until he was able to scramble onto the thick stone wall – then he froze.

Below him was a courtyard, with flaming torches on iron stands which lit up the whole palace. At once he flattened himself along the top of the wall, as voices floated up from only a dozen yards away. He looked down and saw not guards, but two gentlemen in fine clothes, leaning idly against an arched doorway and gossiping.

Heart in mouth, Ben scanned the palace buildings, seeing other doors, but they were further off. His spirits faltered, as he realized there was no means by which he could gain entrance. The moment he jumped down from the wall, he would be seen.

Lying uncomfortably along the stonework, hungry and dirty and afraid, he struggled to think what to do. What he needed now, he thought ruefully, was another of Lady Sarah's "plans". Though even she would have been hard pressed to find a way out of this situation... Then he heard something: something as familiar to him, as it was unexpected.

Through the open doorway where the gentlemen lounged came the distant sound of a lute, skilfully played, and a drum keeping time with it. And as he listened voices rose in song, and his heart leaped as he recognized them: John Symes, Hugh Cotton and Gabriel Tucker – and at once he understood. Lord Bonner's men were entertaining the Queen!

His spirits rose, for now he knew what he must do, and he must do it quickly. With no further attempt at concealment he slid down from the wall and landed on his feet in the courtyard. And as the two gentlemen turned round in surprise, he walked up to them as boldly as Lady Sarah had walked up to the guards at the gate.

"If I might pass through, sirs," he said. "I'm one of Lord Bonner's players."

The men stared at the unkempt urchin in ragged clothes who stood before them. But the next moment, there came voices from nearby. The gentlemen looked – as did Ben – to see Lady Sarah being marched roughly across the courtyard between two scowling guards. Ben gulped, as he realized that whatever tale she had told them had not been believed. Then the guards saw him, and halted.

"There's another of them," one cried. "Grab him!"

But as the two gentlemen turned towards Ben, he ducked and ran between them through the doorway. At his back there were shouts, and the thud of heavy boots, but he did not stop. Along a wide passage he raced, following the sound of the music which was growing louder. In fact, it started to echo around eerily in his head, making him feel dizzy. He had heard of people feeling light-headed through weariness and hunger – was that what was happening to him?

But there was no time to worry about it. Ahead of him was a pair of doors, slightly ajar, from whence came the noise of a great crowd of people. Breathing hard, he reached the doors and shoved them open with all his strength, to enter a wide chamber filled with candlelight. There he stopped, aware of a hundred pairs of eyes suddenly upon him. Then the guards came bursting in behind him, shouting to everyone to clear the way, and the crowd's amazement gave way to cries of alarm. But Ben, his heart thumping, had seen the small platform at the far end of the room, and the figures upon it. And even as they stopped playing and rose from their seats, he ran forward and almost flung himself at their feet.

"It's me – Ben!" he cried. "I've escaped from Bowford with Lady Sarah! There's been murder and plotting, and they've taken Solomon away, and..." Then he stopped, feeling very faint, as the buzz of voices in his ears swelled to a deafening crescendo.

And as he sank to the floor he heard a woman's voice, loud and imperious, issuing a command. He even fancied he saw a tall, red-haired figure with a pale face and a gown that glittered with jewels... then the lights swam dizzily before his eyes, and everything went black.

Chapter Seventeen

*W*hen Ben woke up, he thought for a moment that he was still dreaming. He had been dimly aware of voices, and of being carried, but that seemed a long time ago. Since then he had been troubled by dreams of horsemen chasing him, with swords and pikes...they were trying to get something off him, which was strapped to his chest. Then he sat up wide awake, realizing that he was in bed, undressed, and the plate was gone!

He opened his eyes and bright sunlight stabbed at them, making him blink. Then a figure materialized at his bedside, and relief flooded over him.

"John!"

John Symes was sitting on a stool beside the pallet. He leaned over, smiling. "How are you feeling, master beggar?"

"I...I'm all right, I think," Ben answered uncertainly. "But the plate – where is it?"

"Safe," John answered. "And so are you." He took Ben's hand and squeezed it. "You've had quite an adventure, have you not? We're all mighty proud of you."

A dozen questions rose in Ben's mind, but for the moment he remained silent. He saw that he was in a long, low-roofed attic chamber with pallets along the walls. Scattered about was the familiar baggage of the rest of Lord Bonner's men. He also saw that he had been washed from head to foot, and felt cleaner than he had done for a week.

"Is Lady Sarah all right?" he asked. "Last time I saw her, she was being taken away..."

"She's safe and well," John told him. "Indeed, I hear she's awake already, and asking after you." He paused. "She told us everything, Ben. Last night, before the Queen's servants took her off to wash and attend to her."

"The Queen?" Ben's eyes widened. "Then I did see

her," he muttered, almost to himself. "I thought it was a dream!"

Now, he vividly remembered the tall figure in the candlelit hall, with curly red hair and a lot of jewels... He looked at John and gulped. "You mean, she knows...?"

"She knows all," John answered, "and so does our good Lord Bonner. He had an audience with Her Majesty last night, and took advice from her and from others. There are many noblemen here accompanying the Queen on her progress."

It was all becoming rather a lot for Ben to take in. "What about Solomon?" he asked suddenly.

"The Queen has sent orders to Guildford that Solomon is to be freed at once," John told him. "That rogue of a constable had no right to take him there!"

Ben nodded, then his face clouded. "Lady Sarah's been cruelly used," he said. "And she's worried about her father..."

John's face also grew sombre. "That's another matter," he replied. "I gather the Queen too is concerned for him..." He sat upright. "Still, we'll learn more soon. We're to join His Lordship in an hour, and hear what's to be done. Time enough for you to dress yourself and take some breakfast." He gestured to a little heap of clothes nearby. "We've borrowed some attire for you, off one of the pageboys. Your own clothes were fit only for a bonfire."

Ben managed a smile, feeling a great deal better. But as John rose to his feet, a final thought struck him.

"Tarlton," he muttered. "Is he—"

"Enough!" John raised his hands in mock despair. "There's naught for you to fret about! Now get yourself up and dressed, before the morning's spent!"

An hour later, Ben and the rest of the company gathered in a small downstairs chamber of the palace. Hugh, Gabriel and even Will were so pleased to see him, Ben was quite overwhelmed. But they barely had time to exchange a few words before the door opened and the imposing figure of Lord Bonner himself strode in, followed by several attendants.

Ben had only seen His Lordship once before, in London, soon after he first became apprenticed to the company. But immediately he recognized the portly, handsome man with the neatly trimmed black moustache and beard. His Lordship wore a gold chain over his fine doublet of crimson velvet, a snow-white ruff and a hat with peacock feathers in it. As the players made their bows, their patron inclined his head in return. Then his gaze fell upon Ben.

"Master Button..." His face was stern. "From what I hear, some say you're in need of a sound flogging!"

Ben flinched, then noticed the expressions on the other men's faces, and waited.

"Theft of a valuable golden plate, from Bowford Manor?" Lord Bonner continued. "Do you deny you took it?"

Ben swallowed. "No, My Lord," he replied.

"I rejoice to hear it." His Lordship's sharp eyes bored into Ben's. "And dare I venture that you'd like to see it again?"

Ben did not know what to say. But Lord Bonner turned and beckoned, and a servant stepped forward. He was holding something wrapped in a red cloth... and now Ben saw the smile that spread across His Lordship's face.

"Bring it here," he ordered, stepping over to a small table. "It's time we had a proper look at what has been the cause of so much strife." He gestured to the players. "Will you gather round, my good friends?" As they stepped forward, he turned deliberately to Ben. "You have shown a great deal of courage, master prentice," he said in a gentler tone. "And it's right that you be allowed to share in this moment, as we try to decipher the riddle that's sent certain people into such a frenzy of scheming..." He broke off, and seeing the look on Ben's face, placed a hand on his shoulder.

"I think all will become clear quite soon," he said kindly. "I for one, would never believe for a moment that one of my players stole anything – and certainly not from the house of a gracious host like Sir James Howard! And now, I begin to see what's behind it all..."

Then he turned, as everyone else did, when the door opened again. And Ben's face lit up at the sight of a slight figure in a saffron-coloured gown, her red hair tucked neatly under an embroidered hood.

"Ah...My Lady," Lord Bonner bowed graciously, and Lady Sarah made her curtsey. "Now we're all here, shall we begin?"

Lady Sarah nodded. Briefly her eyes met Ben's. He saw how uneasy she looked, and understood: her mind was on her father, still at Bowford.

But at Lord Bonner's urging, everyone gathered round the table as the servant unwrapped the Lodovico plate. There were murmurs of wonder from the players at the sight of it, but to Ben it was already familiar. He watched His Lordship take the plate in both hands and peer at it.

"Is it true that all this time, your father has been unaware of a cipher, concealed in the design?" he asked Lady Sarah.

"Only Master Henry guessed it, My Lord," Lady Sarah answered. "And I believe he was murdered because of it."

"Well, perhaps his scholarship was not in vain," Lord Bonner said grimly. "I too have some knowledge of the cunning ways in which messages were concealed, in those turbulent years when the Queen of Scots plotted to seize the throne. She's dead these six years, yet our own blessed Queen now awaits the outcome of our little investigation. Let's proceed, shall we?"

Excitement was growing. Everyone pressed forward eagerly as His Lordship turned the plate over, revealing the tracery which Ben and Lady Sarah had examined only the day before, in the derelict barn. As before, they could make out no inscription. But now Lord Bonner put the plate face down on the table, and took a dagger from his belt.

"Master Button – will you hold the plate firm?" he asked.

Ben pressed down on the edges of the plate, as His Lordship bent his head over it, searching for something about its circular base. There were puzzled frowns, for no one could guess what it was he sought. Then at last he pointed.

"There. Do you see?"

Only then did Ben's keen eyes make out a tiny dent in the lip of the plate's base. Without further ado Lord Bonner put the point of his dagger to the gap and pushed it home. Then firmly he levered downwards, causing Ben to put all his weight on the plate to counter his strength...and now came a gasp from the watchers. For with a hiss of escaping air, the false base of the Lodovico plate flew away suddenly, and rolled onto the tabletop with a clang, revealing the true base underneath. And on it, engraved in very small letters, were two columns of words, set closely together.

Lord Bonner signalled to Ben to let go of the plate, and lifted it to show Lady Sarah, who was gazing wide-eyed.

"Your tutor was right," he said softly. "And I am certain as can be that these are the names of sympathizers, mostly Catholics, who would have aided the Queen of Scots in her bid to seize power, in return for rewards and favours after she took the throne! After her execution, the plate was likely stolen by one of her servants, and sold on. It may have passed through several hands before it ended up in the possession of your father, Lady Sarah – who knew nothing of its true purpose. But some who did have stopped at nothing to track it down, knowing full well the danger it poses to those whose names are graven here!"

He peered closely at the list of names, then pointed out one of them to Lady Sarah, who cried out. "Sir Ralph Gosson!"

"Indeed." His Lordship gave a grim smile. "There were always rumours that his loyalty to our Queen was suspect...and if it became known that he was among those who had plotted against her, he would be sent straight to the Tower – and thence to the executioner's block!"

Ben and Lady Sarah looked at each other. Ben gulped to think of the importance of the plate that he had grabbed from Thomas Bullen's hands on the pathway back at Bowford.

"I see why they had to steal it, My Lord," Lady Sarah said quietly, "before my father learned what was on it: for not only Sir Ralph, but Lady Anne too would be disgraced – and my father would never allow her son to inherit Bowford. So I'm certain that Lady Anne too must have known of it, all along..."

She drew a sharp breath, and looked wildly at Lord Bonner. "But now, the Gossons have Father at their mercy!" she cried. "We must go back and save him, before they do something terrible!"

Chapter Eighteen

After that, matters began to move with gathering speed.

Lord Bonner went off, taking Lady Sarah with him, to speak with the Queen in private. Servants hurried about, bearing messages. At last Ben was able to properly rejoin the rest of the company, who were left to their own devices. The five of them went out into the palace gardens to talk matters over.

John and Hugh were filled with remorse for having abandoned Ben and Solomon at Bowford – even though they had been sent packing, with no choice in the matter. It seemed that soon after they reached Oatlands the Queen had arrived, surrounded by courtiers and admirers. The moment she learned that Lord Bonner's celebrated players were in the palace, she had ordered them to provide daily entertainment in the banqueting hall. Their requests for an urgent audience with her had been met with vague promises from harassed royal servants, which led to nothing. All they could do was write letters to Lord Bonner and Sir James. Lord Bonner himself had been delayed, and had not arrived until the previous day. Only now, with Ben and Lady Sarah's dramatic entrance, had the whole tale become known. It was a huge relief to Ben, to know that matters were at last out in the open.

"I haven't stopped fretting about Solomon," John said. "We can only pray he's not been harmed." He looked at Ben. "If it weren't for you, we wouldn't even have known he'd been moved from the brewhouse at Bowford."

"In a way, I'm glad they moved him again," Ben said, recalling The Pig's house at Cobham, and the lock-up behind it. "He's well out of the clutches of Piggott and his man."

He shuddered, and Hugh put an arm about him. "Well, you're safe now," he said. "And when Solomon gets here, we can get back on the road and leave all these troubles behind us – eh, John?"

John said nothing, and the others looked at him.

"There's no reason for us to stay is there?" Gabriel enquired. "Now the theft's been cleared up, I mean…"

"His Lordship wants us to wait until he's spoken with Her Majesty," John answered.

"More hanging about?" Will Sanders grunted. "What for?"

John shrugged, then saw that Ben was looking around. "Where are the stables?" he asked. "I'd like to go and see Tarlton."

"I'll take you," Will said, and led the way.

When they arrived, the Oatlands stable yard was a hive of activity. Grooms scurried about saddling horses, and men-at-arms in helmets stood in a stern-looking group, talking among themselves. Ben and Will had to thread their way through into the stable. But there in a corner was Tarlton, and Ben hurried to greet him, ruffling his mane while he talked softly to the old horse. He was still there some minutes later, when a voice behind made him look round quickly.

"I wanted to thank you," Lady Sarah said.

Ben bowed low. "You honour me, My Lady." Then he saw how pale and tense she looked.

"I'll never forget what you've done," she said.

Ben smiled and shook his head. "I couldn't have got the plate here without you," he told her.

She managed a quick smile in return, then asked: "Do you have everything you need?"

"To be with my company again is enough," Ben replied. "Once Solomon's restored to us, we can be on our way."

"That's well." She watched him stroking Tarlton for a little while. "The Queen has ordered soldiers to go straight to Bowford, and arrest Uncle Ralph and Master Bullen," she told him. "I'm following later with Lord Bonner."

"I'm sure all will be well, in the end," Ben said.

But Lady Sarah's face had clouded. "I'm not sure of it at all," she said. "You don't know Lady Anne."

"Surely, now the truth's out about the plate, and the list of names," he began, but Lady Sarah was shaking her head.

"I believe she'll deny all knowledge of the list," she said. "She'll let Uncle Ralph take the blame. From what Lord Bonner says, he's in debt from gambling. Lady Anne will say it was he who had the plate stolen to pay his debts. She's always been able to make my father believe whatever she wants him to."

Ben looked downcast. "Then what's to be done?" he asked.

Lady Sarah shrugged. "So long as I can be with my father again, I no longer care," she said.

From outside came the sound of stamping hooves and jangling harness, as the soldiers got themselves mounted. Lady Sarah started to go, but to Ben's surprise she turned back, ran forward and gave him a hug. Then without a word, she hurried outside.

Ben thought hard about what she had said. For some reason, he felt empty inside. Suddenly he found himself thinking of the old dog, Brutus, and realized how much he had missed him. At last he said farewell to Tarlton and came out of the stable, to find Will watching the men-at-arms ride away. Led by one of the Queen's captains, they clattered out of the yard towards the palace gates. There was no sign of Lady Sarah.

Late in the afternoon Solomon Tree arrived at Oatlands on horseback, escorted by two of the Queen's guards.

The company were waiting anxiously for him in the courtyard. To their relief he had not been hurt, though he was tired and weak, and in need of fresh clothes. He had withstood his ordeal with the usual gloominess, as he now accepted his release.

"The jail at Guildford's foul," he told them, after they had all gathered about, clapping him on the back. "And the food's worse. I told them I'd seen pigs fed better, and after that one of the guards started snorting whenever he went by. I managed to give him a smirk when they let me out."

The others were grinning, pleased to see that he was the same old Solomon. Later, when he had heard the tale of Ben's adventures over a supper in the palace kitchens, Solomon fixed him with one of his hangdog looks.

"He'll be wanting an increase in his wages," he said to John Symes, "seeing how clever he's been." Then he noticed Ben's thoughtful expression. "Yet, there's something on your mind, isn't there?"

Ben was silent. When the others looked at him, he told them quickly what Lady Sarah had said to him in the stable: about Lady Anne, and how she would try to talk her way out of everything. When he had finished, there was a pause.

"I don't see what we can do," Will Sanders said with a shrug. "Shouldn't we be on our way?"

"I won't be sorry to put all this business behind us, and get back on the road," Gabriel added.

They looked to John, who said: "I spoke with His Lordship before he left for Bowford. We can leave whenever we like. There are plenty of noblemen heading home to their country houses for the summer who would be glad to have us entertain them. Especially as we've just been performing for the Queen."

Then he waited. The others glanced at each other, but Solomon had not taken his eyes off Ben. "What does our young prentice say?" he asked. Before Ben could answer, he said to John: "I believe we owe him a debt. It's thanks to him I'm a free man, isn't it?"

John nodded. "Speak up, Ben."

Ben looked round at each of them. "Well, I've got a notion," he said. "In fact, it's more of a plan…"

At sunrise the following day, a heavily laden cart drawn by an old chestnut horse rumbled out of the palace gates. But instead of taking the westward road towards Weybridge as expected, the cart turned south, in the direction of Cobham. Those who saw the players depart wondered if they had taken the wrong road; then they quickly forgot about it and returned to their business. What did a troupe of travelling rogues matter, compared to the work of attending Queen Elizabeth?

Lord Bonner's Men travelled the few miles to Cobham in silence. Once again Will drove the cart while the others went ahead on foot. To Ben, who had walked this road mainly in darkness, the way looked unfamiliar. But when they passed a broken-down barn set back from the road, he knew it was where he and Lady Sarah had sheltered. It seemed like an age ago. Only later did he remember that he had left his pack there; he never did recover it.

They passed through Cobham without incident, and climbed the road towards Bowford. Soon they topped the hill, and the great house with its paddock and outbuildings was spread out before them. They reached the gate, but no one challenged them, even when they entered the stable yard and Will drew the cart to a halt.

The place was eerily quiet. Where were the men-at-arms who had ridden out from Oatlands? Will got down, and all of them stared about. Ben was nervous, remembering his dash for freedom some nights back. Then he felt a hand on his shoulder, and was cheered by the faces of John Symes and Hugh Cotton. Their looks said it plainly: no one was going to split Lord Bonner's Men up this time. The six of them drew close together, and at a word from John they walked out of the stables into the kitchen gardens.

Now there came a shout, and they turned to see a figure hurrying towards them. Ben broke into a smile at the sight of someone he had almost forgotten about: Ned Stiles. He stepped forward eagerly, then halted. For Ned's expression was one of alarm.

"Master Ben – what are you doing back here?"

As the players gathered round him, the young falconer looked startled, until John Symes raised a hand. "We mean you no harm," he said. "What's happened? Where are the soldiers?"

Ned addressed Ben. "There's been mayhem here," he said. "Sir Ralph and Master Bullen have fled – heading for the south coast I heard, with the Queen's men chasing after them!"

Now Ned began to speak readily, as if glad to have someone to talk to. "Sir Ralph and Bullen were leading search parties all over the county, after you and Lady Sarah took off. But they came back empty handed..." He looked at Ben with admiration. "How did you manage to hide from them?"

But John was impatient. "I fear we've no time for traveller's tales," he said. "We must find Lord Bonner. Do you know where he is?"

Ned shrugged. "Somewhere about...Lady Anne received him yesterday. They say she's mighty upset at everything."

"What of Sir James?" Ben asked anxiously.

"He's sick," Ned told him, with a shake of his head. "No one knows what's wrong with him. Lady Anne won't let anyone else attend him, not even a physician. But I hear Lady Sarah's with him now – she said she'd jump out of a window if they didn't let her in his chamber! Even Lady Anne couldn't stop her!"

The others glanced at John Symes, who took a deep breath. "Well," he said. "Shall we make our entrance?"

They turned towards the house, and Ben threw Ned a smile before moving off.

Soon after, having at last been challenged by a couple of startled manservants, the company were ushered into Sir James's private chamber. And here, behind the table scattered with documents, sat Lady Anne and her son Giles. The mistress of Bowford appeared calm, but her expression was icy as she fixed her gaze upon John Symes.

"How dare you intrude here at a time like this?" she asked sharply. "What is it you want?"

But she looked startled when John put on a broad smile.

"Why, we've come to give a special performance, My Lady," he replied, "by order of the Queen!"

Lady Anne stared at him. "A performance?" she echoed. "With my husband on his sick bed upstairs… Has he not suffered enough, with all the treachery that has been revealed here?"

Ben's heart was thumping. Had he not known better, he would have believed that Lady Anne knew nothing of the plot to steal the Lodovico plate. He saw her look of deep concern, as if Sir James was all she cared about. Some people, he decided, could act better than any professional! He swallowed, then saw to his surprise that John was rather enjoying the moment.

"But My Lady, that's precisely why the Queen has ordered it," John told her. "We suggested it to our patron Lord Bonner at Oatlands, and he thought it a splendid idea – as did the Queen. The best way to cheer Sir James – to lift his spirits, as she put it – would be for him to watch Lord Bonner's Men give a show. Better than any medicine, she said!"

At that, Lady Anne paled. And now Ben glanced at Giles, who had so far ignored him. He threw Ben a look of hatred that would have made a lesser boy flinch. But Ben merely met his eye, and looked away.

"It's out of the question!" Lady Anne snapped, finding her voice at last. "Now I will have my steward escort you to the gates and send you on your way..." She broke off, for Giles had leaned forward to whisper in her ear. Perhaps, Ben thought, he was reminding her that their steward was no longer here.

"Yes, yes!" Lady Anne hissed, and Giles lapsed into a sullen silence. But at that moment the door opened, and the players breathed sighs of relief: Lord Bonner had arrived at last.

"Ah! There you are!" Smiling broadly, their patron swept into the room, pausing only to make his bow to Lady Anne. "Making plans for the performance already? Splendid!"

"But – My Lord, surely this is not the time..." Lady Anne faltered, and Ben's heart lifted. Hope surged through him that his plan might have a chance of succeeding. And now, the other players were starting to smile at each other.

"Best treat Sir James could have, My Lady," Lord Bonner went on briskly. "I've just come from his bedchamber, and he swears he's well enough to come down for the show."

Lady Anne stood up, frowning. "You've been to his chamber...?"

His Lordship was nodding. "Lady Sarah let me in. Once she knew it was me, she was glad to unlock the door." His smile had faded now. "She's taken the precaution of throwing away the cordial you've been dosing Sir James with," he added. "I thought her very wise, for it doesn't seem to do him much good, does it? Just keeps sending him to sleep."

The players stared hard at Lady Anne, who sat down abruptly. Had she truly been giving some sleeping potion to her husband? That would be one way of keeping him to his bed, Ben thought, while the "plotters" hunted for him and Lady Sarah... He almost gasped at the wickedness of it.

"Well then, that's settled!" Lord Bonner's smile was back. "My company will give a wondrous show tonight in the Great Hall, improvised specially for the occasion. Everyone will be invited, from far and wide!" He turned to his troupe and clapped his hands. "You'd better go and start preparing, hadn't you? You must have lots to do. I know I have!"

The players made their bows and left the chamber. Ben glanced back and saw Lady Anne sitting motionless. Beside her Giles was biting his nails, staring down at the table. This time he did not look up. It was as if he knew that the tide had at last turned against his mother and uncle – and against him, too.

Chapter Nineteen

That evening, the great hall was packed to the doors.

Backstage, all was bustle. From behind the same curtain that had been rigged the week before, Ben peeped out at the audience. Sir James, muffled in a heavy cloak and looking pale, was seated in the centre with Lady Sarah at his side, and Lord Bonner close by. On the other side Lady Anne sat, stiff and upright, with Giles. Other nobles, gentlemen and ladies from the surrounding countryside who had been invited by Lord Bonner, were talking cheerfully among themselves. Servants and attendants made up the rest of the crowd. None of them, Ben knew, had any inkling of the true purpose of this performance. He took some deep breaths, gathering his courage. He had never felt so nervous in his whole life.

Then he stiffened: for seated near the doors was none other than William Piggott the constable. Lord Bonner, Ben knew, had ordered him to attend, which was why The Pig looked so uneasy, and kept taking generous swigs from a goblet clutched in his fist. Ben's eyes roved past him...and stopped. Sitting near The Pig, staring about suspiciously, was his henchman Nat.

But there was no time to think about them, for John Symes, his lute slung about his neck, was calling the company together. Solomon had his drum, and Hugh and Gabriel had recorders. Ben lined up with the others, and, at John's signal, Will threw back the curtain. Lord Bonner's Men were on!

The applause was enthusiastic, for His Lordship had spread the word that his troupe came hotfoot from entertaining the Queen. And as they launched into "Fine Knacks for Ladies", Ben knew that this would be a night to remember. Then the player in him took over, and for a while at least he forgot who was watching, and looked to his performance.

They sang old favourites, their six voices in harmony, from Ben's treble to Will's bass: "Three Ravens", "Oh Mistress Mine", and "Now is the Month of Maying". They played "The Honeysuckle" on lute and recorders. Then they danced a galliard, and finally a set of jigs, each one faster and more furious than the last, until the audience were on their feet, beating time and shouting their approval. When it ended, and the players took their bows, sweating and breathless, the clapping and cheering was like a torrent of noise that swept over them.

But now it was time to put Ben's plan into action.

John Symes stepped forward, smiling, raising his hands to quell the applause. "My Lords, Ladies and gentlemen," he called out, "we have an addition to our entertainment tonight – something very special. We have prepared a little play, based on a true tale of murder and treachery, that will strike terror into all your hearts!"

Some of the guests *oohed* in mock fright, laughing to one another. Others, however, who had heard something about recent events at Bowford Manor, looked rather uneasy. But after exchanging a few looks they settled back to watch, as the players disappeared behind their curtain. The lights began to dim, and people looked round to see servants snuffing out some of the candles. Then everyone fell silent, as a figure appeared – and at once there was a murmur from many throats.

The man was a servant in Bowford livery, played by Will Sanders. But the reason the watchers began muttering among themselves, was that he carried the Lodovico plate.

Peering about furtively, Will hurried to the nearest table, startling several gentlemen and ladies. As they watched he grabbed a handful of fruit from a bowl, and spread it on the precious plate. Then he stood upright like a servingman, and bearing the plate before him, carried it sedately away, towards the curtain.

Now another figure appeared, in an apron and hood, and a gasp of recognition went up from the Bowford servants: it was a washerwoman, carrying a basket of linen. And she was being played by Ben Button.

At once Ben took the plate from Will and hid it in the basket. Then he and Will hurried off with it.

A deadly silence had fallen. In the middle of the hall, Sir James half rose from his chair. But Lady Sarah, wide-eyed with excitement, put a hand on his arm and he sat down again, as another character entered.

This was clearly a nobleman, who strutted forward, slapping his thigh impatiently with a riding glove. But before the watchers could put a name to him, it was spelled out for them. For another man, with a steward's keys on a chain about his neck, arrived to join him. "Sir Ralph!" he cried. "Now we have the plate we must get it away, before it is discovered!"

An intake of breath went up from the crowd. But in the speech that followed, they fell silent again. For the two men – played by Hugh Cotton and Gabriel Tucker – proceeded to spell out clearly to everyone, the story of what had happened to the Lodovico plate.

They told how it had been sent to the Queen of Scots in her imprisonment, as a gift – but one that carried a cipher: a hidden list of sympathizers, who would help her seize the throne when she made her bid for power. But when they mentioned names, a wave of unease swept through the audience. For among them, was that of Sir Ralph Gosson.

Now, one might have heard a pin drop. Gazes shifted towards Lady Anne, who sat in her chair like stone. But then Ben, as the washerwoman, hurried on again, very agitated. "Sirs," he cried, "we are undone!"

All eyes upon him, he told the two men that their plan had been discovered. "It's thanks to Lady Sarah, and that meddling boy player!" Ben cried. "They've told her tutor, Master Henry. He knows too much. The fellow must be silenced before he tells Sir James!"

Then Gabriel, as Bullen, turned deliberately to the audience. "There's one man who'll know how to deal with the matter!" he snarled. "Where's that sot of a constable – Piggott, are you there? I need someone despatched, and quickly!"

There was a moment's silence; then several things happened.

First came a commotion from the middle of the hall, and people looked round in alarm to see that Lady Anne had fainted. Giles sprang to her side, his face deathly pale.

But at once there was another commotion, from near the doors. And people looked round to see The Pig on his feet, swaying drunkenly. As they watched, he raised a trembling finger and pointed it at the players.

"You lie!" The Pig shouted, plainly terrified. "I've killed no one. I didn't want any part of that!" He whirled about and pointed at Nat, who jumped to his feet.

"'Twas that fool, there!" The Pig shouted. "He was told to frighten the tutor so he'd keep his mouth shut – not drown him! He took him to the pond, and held him underwater too long! He wasn't supposed to kill him!"

Chapter Twenty

The Pig stared about wild-eyed as the crowd gaped, looking from him to Nat and back again. Then The Pig saw the danger – but too late.

With a cry of animal rage Nat sprang at him, one hand going to his belt. There were screams of terror as his dagger rose, glittering in the candlelight...then came a groan, as it was plunged into The Pig's chest. But even as the constable slumped to the floor, Nat was running through the crowd, shoving people aside. And now, there was uproar.

First he ran to the rear doors of the great hall, then

stopped: for several gentlemen, bolder than the rest, were on their feet and hurrying to block his way. So he turned and ran like a hare to the other end of the hall, where the players still stood. Diving past them, he tore at the entrance curtain, pulling it down.

But in his way stood John Symes, Will Sanders and Solomon Tree.

Crouching, Nat faced them. "Move!" he cried. "I'll slay any man who tries to stop me!"

Then his head snapped round, for someone was moving up behind him: Hugh, the company's sword-fighting expert. And in his hand was a silver-handled rapier.

"Drop the dagger and kneel," Hugh ordered, stepping in Nat's way. "Or I shall be obliged to wound you."

"You? You're but a player!" Nat snarled. "A fake! Get out of my way, or—"

"Or what?" Will had moved to stand by Hugh. And beside him appeared Gabriel, who was still in the role of Bullen. To Nat's dismay the little man puffed out his chest and pointed at him. "On your knees, villain!" he snapped. "You're under arrest!"

Nat was looking confused. He whirled about like a hunted animal, holding the blood-stained dagger before him. But to his dismay the players did not shrink back. Instead they surrounded him. They seemed to have forgotten the audience, who were watching this new scene unfold in shocked silence. But this was no play – it was real!

"I mean it!" Nat shouted. He lunged at Gabriel with his dagger – and connected with nothing but empty air. For Gabriel had sidestepped with lightning speed, and stuck his foot out. With a cry, Nat fell forward. At once he tried to scramble up, but he fell back and finally lay still. For the tip of Hugh's rapier was pressed tight against his throat.

There Nat stayed, looking balefully up at Hugh and cursing under his breath, as men in Bowford livery hurried up at last to disarm him. As he was dragged roughly to his feet, Hugh smiled at him, and gripping the end of the rapier, bent it like a stick of willow.

"You're right: he's only a player," Solomon Tree said in a mournful voice. "And it's only a *dancing rapier* – an ornamental sword, see? It wouldn't hurt a puppy, though it might serve to stick a louse, like you."

Then he moved aside as, watched by everyone, Nat was taken away, scowling and cursing under his breath.

The players stood in a circle and gazed at each

other, exhilarated after all the excitement. Further away, a crowd had gathered about Sir James and Lady Anne. A smaller group was clustered about The Pig, who lay still where he had fallen. Ben's heart was pounding. But he grew calmer as John put a hand on his shoulder.

"Well, your plan seems to have worked," he said.

"It wouldn't have, without all of you," Ben told him breathlessly.

"Do you think there'll be any sort of reward?" Will Sanders asked. "For exposing a murderer like we did?"

John put on a wry smile. "I'll speak to His Lordship," he began, then broke off, for Lord Bonner himself was hurrying towards them.

"All I want's a good supper, a cup of wine and a soft bed," Solomon muttered, not having noticed his approach. "Shouldn't be too much to ask His Lordship, should it, after we've just stared death in the face? I suppose he thinks it's all in a day's work..." Then he saw the others' expressions, and gulped.

"He's behind me, isn't he?" he said.

Ben nodded, feeling a grin tugging at the corners of his mouth. But he put on a serious face, and turned to make his bow to their patron.

*

The next morning dawned, bright and sunny. But Ben Button had been lying awake for some time, thinking over all the events of last night. Murder and mayhem, in a hall full of people... Not to mention the capture of the villainous Nat. It seemed like a dream – but he knew well enough that it wasn't. Today was the day after Lord Bonner's Men had performed their improvised play *The Golden Plate* – which would not only be the talk of Bowford Manor, but of the whole of Surrey for years to come.

Ben had slept soundly, as had all the players. And when they rose from their beds and came down to take breakfast, they were taken aback to find themselves treated like heroes by the kitchen servants. Ben was doubly surprised when Master Lamb, looking somewhat subdued, came over to speak to him.

"I ask your pardon," the cook said, "if you were dealt with harshly here. Though I never thought you a thief, as some did."

"I know," Ben said. He smiled, but Master Lamb did not.

"You made but one mistake in your little play last night," the cook said thoughtfully. "It wasn't a servingman who took the gold plate from the hall: it was Jane."

When Ben showed his surprise, he went on: "I guessed it, after you acted it out. She was clearing away that night, and with all the coming and going, she must have slipped the plate out the back door to Nan. You got that part right. They were always thick as thieves, those two. Seems they were paid by Bullen..." He shook his head. "They've run away of course, but I've spoken with Sir James. He'll know what to do."

He sighed. "I thought all my kitchen folk were honest. But Jane's a sly one, like her father. He's one of the grooms – the surly fellow. You know him? Anyway he's fled, too!"

Ben nodded. And with that, the cook patted him on the shoulder. "I'll have a food basket made up for you to take on your way," he said to the other players. "It'll be as good as a feast, I promise." Then he moved off, and began shouting at the turnspit boy.

Solomon watched him go. "His name's Lamb, isn't it?" he murmured. "I thought he looked a bit sheepish..."

Soon after, feeling more cheerful than they had in a long while, the company gathered in the stable yard. The cart was packed, and Will was about to lead Tarlton out, when one of the grooms hurried up with a message: they were summoned to the house by Sir James.

A few minutes later they were facing him in his private chamber; but there was a very different atmosphere from when they had last stood before him. For one thing, Lord Bonner was there too, pacing about briskly. And Ben's heart warmed to see Lady Sarah sitting beside her father, looking happier than he had ever seen her. She caught his eye, then lowered her gaze as her father addressed them.

"I have much to thank you all for," Sir James began. He still looked pale, but there was a glint in his eye which Ben had not seen before. And he knew, as did the others, that the master of Bowford was on the road to recovery. It cheered them to see it.

As if he had read their thoughts, Sir James said: "As you may see, my health is improving – and perhaps my senses are, too." He glanced at Lady Sarah, then added: "I have been foolish. I was blinded to what was happening here under my own roof. Indeed, I nearly lost not only Bowford, but everything that is precious to me!"

He broke off, and put a hand to his forehead. The players were silent, before Lord Bonner spoke up. He was smiling slightly, but his tone was grave.

"You have saved Sir James from ruin, my friends,"

he said. "Or rather, Lady Sarah and Master Button have – with a little help from the rest of us." He glanced at Ben, who looked at the floor in embarrassment.

"It's true." Lord Bonner nodded. "For if Sir James had become so weak that his reason left him, he might well have signed the papers that Lady Anne had drawn up, signing Bowford Manor away to her own son Giles. Since he is not of age, Lady Anne would have been mistress of Bowford – and shared her new wealth with her brother. Sir Ralph would have been able to pay his gambling debts, and in time, of course, Giles would have inherited everything."

Lady Sarah looked up and met Ben's eye. He nodded slowly, remembering what she had told him when they first met.

"May we ask what's become of them, sir?" John Symes asked. "Lady Anne, I mean, and—"

"She's been taken to London, to the Tower," Lord Bonner answered. "The Queen is even now being told of the whole matter. She will see justice done. As it will be to Sir Ralph too, and Master Bullen," he added. "I'm certain Her Majesty's guards will catch up with them before they can find a ship to make their escape."

"And the constable?" John enquired.

"Dead," His Lordship replied grimly. "And his murderer, Nat, will go to the gallows. I doubt if the people of Cobham will miss either of them."

Though Ben had questions of his own, he kept a respectful silence. Then he saw Sir James looking at him.

"Perhaps Master Button would like to know that Giles is confined to his chamber for the present," he said. "I know you did not steal his dagger – indeed, I suspected it even before we discovered the true culprit: a certain groom who was paid by Giles to slip the dagger into your belongings."

He sighed. "As Lord Bonner said, Giles is not of age," he went on. "I gave him the choice of remaining at Bowford as my ward, provided he would try to mend his ways. But his mother has begged he be allowed to go to London, so he can visit her in the Tower... It seems she cannot bear to be parted from him. And since he wants to go, perhaps it's best."

Sir James reached out and took his daughter's hand, and his expression was grim. "As for Henry Godfrey," he said, "he was a good man, and a wise one. His death will always be on my conscience. He had no family of his own, so he will be buried here, with all honour."

Then at last he smiled feebly at Lady Sarah, and it

was as if a cloud had lifted from them both. He turned back to the players.

"You have reunited me with my daughter, Ben Button," Sir James said quietly. "And you will not go unrewarded."

He took a purse from his gown, and held it out. The players glanced at each other, hearing the chink of coins. Lord Bonner nodded to Ben to step forward.

"They called you rogues," Sir James said, addressing them all. "But the true rogues were here at Bowford, all along. Take your reward in gold with my blessing. And if you pass this way again, you will always be welcome to perform under my roof – though I hope you will not need to make up another play to show me the error of my ways!"

Ben took the purse and bowed, lost for words. The other players followed suit; it was time to leave. They made their farewells, and filed out of the chamber for the last time. But despite the praise ringing in his ears, Ben's heart was heavy. For though he glanced at Lady Sarah, she kept her gaze on the table before her, and did not look up.

A short while later Ben stood beside Tarlton, patting his neck while Will climbed into the driver's seat.

Then the players left the stable yard, as Will shook the reins and Tarlton began to walk, the cart rumbling over the cobbles. Ben walked alongside it.

But as they cleared the yard and skirted the paddock, heading for the gates, there came a chorus of voices. Ben turned, and was surprised to see Tom Beech and the rest of the gardeners gathering in a body beside the path. Will stopped the cart, and the others hung back to watch as Beech strolled over to Ben.

"Snakes and lizards, boy," the old gardener wheezed. "You wasn't going to steal away without saying goodbye, were ye?"

"Of course not." Ben smiled, and took the gnarled hand that was thrust towards him. After shaking Ben's hand up and down a few times, Beech turned to the prentices. One of them came up and held out a large jar.

"Honey – the best of my crop," Beech said. "You'll need it to sweeten your dinner."

Ben thanked him, took the jar and handed it to Will. He felt subdued: not so long ago, he couldn't wait to escape from Bowford Manor. Now, he found himself sorry to leave.

"Goodbye, Master Beech," he said. But Beech and the others were already walking off, back to their never-ending work in the gardens. At the archway the old man waved, then disappeared.

Will whistled to Tarlton, and the cart rumbled on. They passed through the gates and out onto the road, the other players talking easily among themselves. But still Ben had a lump in his throat, that stubbornly refused to go away. He remembered leaving London, which seemed a long time ago now, and feeling the same when he looked back at Brutus. It would be the end of the summer before he saw the old hound again... He sighed, and tried to put the thought to the back of his mind.

Then he started, as something flew past him with a whirr of wings. Shading his eyes, he peered as the falcon climbed skywards, to hang motionless in the clear air above him. And he looked round, to see Ned Stiles come running.

"Joan's frisky today," the falconer's boy said, out of breath. "I'm hard pressed to keep up with her." He stopped, facing Ben, as if suddenly short of words.

Ben smiled at him. "If you ever come to London..." he began, but Ned shook his head.

"Me, in London?" he echoed. "I'd get lost in five minutes!"

He held out his hand, and Ben took it, surprised at the strength of the other boy's grip. There was suddenly a lot he wanted to say, but somehow he didn't know where to begin; and Ned was already starting to go. But at the last moment, he turned and threw Ben a wide grin.

"By the heavens," Ned said. "I'll never forget the look on Master Giles's face that day, when you shoved him into the stream! Not as long as I live, I won't!"

Then he ran off, following his falcon. Ben turned away, and found himself smiling.

They passed along the road, and began to descend the long slope towards Cobham. They would cross the river, John had said, and make for the next town, where they might perform on the green if the townsfolk would let them. The sun was climbing, and a long day's travel stretched before them. But despite his sadness at leaving, Ben found an odd stirring of excitement within him. What further adventures might await him in the months and years ahead, with Lord Bonner's Men?

He sighed, fixing his gaze on the dusty road...and listened. And then he stiffened, for there was no mistaking the sound of galloping hooves... He whirled round, shielding his eyes from the sun's rays. There was a blur of grey, and he saw a dappled pony, racing up alongside. And as Will Sanders looked round in his seat, the pony sped past them towards the hill above Bowford Manor, from where the rider could look down to the valley of the River Mole and beyond.

And though the lump in his throat was still there, Ben's spirits lifted. For the rider was a slight figure with red hair which had come loose, so that it flew behind her in the breeze. She was wearing an old green gown, and waving at him...and he knew she would be sitting on the hilltop watching him, until he was out of sight.

ELIZABETHAN MYSTERIES

False Fire

Lord Bonner's men are performing at the Rose
Theatre in London, but all is not running smoothly.
Strange things keep happening – costumes and props
go missing, the theatre almost catches fire – until
finally it seems that someone's life may be in
real danger.

Ben Button is determined to discover who is
behind the lethal dirty tricks campaign. But as
he gets deeper into his investigations, he finds
himself embroiled in a murky, cut-throat world
of corruption...

Look out for Ben Button's new mystery adventure,
False Fire.

About the author

John Pilkington worked in a research laboratory, on a farm, and as a rock guitarist in several bands before realizing he wanted to write. After taking a degree in Drama and English, and acting and directing for a touring theatre company, he began his professional writing career with radio plays. He has since written plays for the theatre and television scripts for the BBC. He is also the author of a series of historical crime novels, and a non-fiction book, *A Survival Guide for Writers*. *Rogues' Gold* is his first book for younger readers.

Born in Lancashire, John now lives in Devon with his partner and son.

Usborne Quicklinks

For links to websites where you can find out more about the Elizabethan spy network, learn about plots to overthrow Queen Elizabeth I and explore the life of a boy actor, go to the Usborne Quicklinks Website at www.usborne-quicklinks.com and enter the keywords "rogues' gold".

Internet safety

When using the Internet, make sure you follow these safety guidelines:

- Ask an adult's permission before using the Internet.
- Never give out personal information, such as your name, address or telephone number.
- If a website asks you to type in your name or email address, check with an adult first.
- If you receive an email from someone you don't know, don't reply to it.

Usborne Publishing is not responsible and does not accept liability for the availability or content of any website other than its own, or for any exposure to harmful, offensive, or inaccurate material which may appear on the Web. Usborne Publishing will have no liability for any damage or loss caused by viruses that may be downloaded as a result of browsing the sites it recommends. We recommend that children are supervised while on the Internet.

For more heart-pounding
historical adventures
log on to
www.fiction.usborne.com

GRAHAM MARKS

Snatched!

Daniel never knew his real parents – abandoned in a lion's cage as a baby, he was adopted into Hubble's travelling circus. When he suffers terrible visions of the future he desperately tries to change what he sees. But he cannot avoid being snatched away to London, where it seems he may have the chance to unlock the riddle of his past. Will he like the answers he finds?

Action-packed, filled with drama and excitement, *Snatched!* takes you on a helter-skelter journey – from the breathtaking theatrics of the circus ring to the very real perils lurking on the streets of Victorian London.

"A hugely enjoyable read with a memorable cast."
The Bookseller

0 7460 6840 9

ANDREW MATTHEWS

The Shadow Garden

Matty's sixth sense tells her that Tagram House is harbouring a dark secret. The master, Dr. Hobbes, seems charming on the surface but underneath Matty detects a glint of razor-sharp steel. Her fears lead Matty to the eerie Shadow Garden, and she eventually discovers what's buried there. Now she must untangle the mystery before disaster engulfs everyone.

Like cold fingers reaching from the grave, a chilling atmosphere of mystery and suspense seeps through the pages of this haunting ghost story.

"This is a highly atmospheric novel...a satisfying, gripping read with a truly alarming climax."
School Librarian

0 7460 6794 1

MALCOLM ROSE

Kiss of Death

On a school trip to the plague village of Eyam, Seth is moved by the story of how villagers sacrficed their lives to the dreaded Black Death. Kim and Wes are more interested in what they see at the bottom of the wishing well – money!

But when they snatch the coins they also pick up something they hadn't bargained for, and as the hideous consequences of their theft catch up with them all, Seth is forced to face a terrifying truth. Has Eyam's plague-ridden past resurfaced to seek revenge?

Past and present collide in this exciting thriller by acclaimed author, Malcolm Rose.

0 7460 7064 0